FOR THE
LOVE
OF A
WITCH

A FAIRY TALE BY

Sarah-Jane Lehoux

FOR THE LOVE OF A WITCH
© Sarah-Jane Lehoux 2020

First edition ● October 2020
ISBN Print: 978-0-9881456-1-0
ISBN EBook: 978-0-9881456-0-3

Edited by Roisin Heycock
Cover Image by Tithi Luadthong
Cover Design by Sarah-Jane Lehoux
Interior Design by Sarah-Jane Lehoux

I met a lady in the meads,
Full beautiful – a faery's child;
Her hair was long, her foot was light,
And her eyes were wild.

John Keats, *La Belle Dame sans Merci*

PROLOGUE

 nce upon a time, in a kingdom of silver trees and golden meadows, crystal waters and diamond skies, a Beast was born from fire and rock and hate. He was a foul, nameless horror that coveted the beauty of the world above, wishing to both possess and destroy it. Aeons passed under the watch of his unblinking eye, for although his body was that of a monster, he had a tactician's mind and the greed of a soulless and predatory child. He plumbed fathomless depths of darkest imagination, plotting wicked schemes while amassing the strength of centuries until finally, having grown to the point that he had no mortal equal, he ripped himself free from the belly of the earth.

His rise to power was an indulgent game. There were no limits to his cruelty, no misery he wasn't ecstatic to inflict. He devoured all he desired, leaving little more than ash in his wake. A brave few tested their courage against the Beast, yet neither blade nor arrow could pierce his ancient hide. No spell slowed his devil's pace. Armies fled, castles crumbled, and the people were abandoned to his mercy, though of course he had none.

Then one night, after even the memory of hope had died, a single scream, more piteous than any that came before, rang out through the moonless sky. The scream was a pact, a treaty signed with virgin blood. Content at last, the Beast slithered back underground, and there he stayed.

Years went by. The world should have begun to heal, to forget the Beast and his crimes as one forgets a nightmare upon waking to the safety of daylight. Yet this did not happen. He wouldn't allow it. He did not stir from his lair, no, but the damage he wrought would not be undone. Evil leached from him as he slept, corrupting all it touched. As the land itself twisted into his likeness, desperation drove the survivors of his tyrannical rule into madness and savagery. They plundered, pillaged, branded, and burned without fear of reprisal, for in truth, there was no one left to stand against them.

The chaos spread, as chaos is wont to do, eventually spilling across the border of the neighbouring kingdom. Then did Queen Muireann summon her court to discuss what had come to be known as the Accursed Lands. Assembled from all corners of her realm, these well-born men, adorned in colourful finery and elegant manners, went round and round the issue.

"We must act immediately," said those closest to the

turmoil.

"We mustn't charge headlong into war," said those who were furthest away.

Hours inched into days, yet still, a consensus could not be reached. The finery drooped. Manners took on a much less appealing form.

While her court echoed with opinion, Muireann sat frozen in tongue-tied dismay. She'd been just a maid of fourteen when the crown was placed upon her fair head, and because of this, she had relied heavily, too heavily, on the counsel of her advisors for the whole of her reign. They had more than her trust; they had her utter dependence. With these same advisors squabbling amongst themselves like a gaggle of ganders, she was at a loss, very nearly reverting to the small, inconsolable girl she was when her father the King had suddenly died of fever.

From across the room, one man worried over her every frown. Eoin, the newly knighted son of Sir Ualtar, had loved Muireann since they played together as children. Even though they'd always understood he was too far beneath her for her to return his affections, he never quite persuaded his heart to believe it, and she dreaded the day he would. He was her shadow, her confidant, the hand that steadied her, and the ear that held her secrets.

I have to help her, he thought, as her mouth trembled in warning of tears. *Somehow, I have to save her.*

As if he'd called out her name, she turned towards him. "What say you, Sir Eoin?"

Her question, although softly spoken, quieted the impassioned gentry. Their attention fell to Eoin, and its weight settled uncomfortably onto his shoulders.

"My Queen?" he mumbled, only to have his foot crushed under his father's heel.

"I've noticed you haven't said your piece, Sir, and would be most grateful to hear it."

His father's heel dug in further. Beating back a wince, Eoin cleared his throat. He poured a glass of wine and drank it slowly, gaining precious seconds to think. He knew what his father wanted. Ualtar had recommended the construction of a fortified wall between the two kingdoms. A foolish plan. Something as simple as a wall couldn't stave off the advances of famine and disease, and Eoin couldn't in good conscience pretend that it would. Yet that was precisely what was expected of him. Ualtar had no care for Eoin's conscience. He was a difficult man, proud and petty. Anything less than total deference to his will would be considered an act of treason.

"My Queen, the wall…"

He stopped. Glancing at his father, Eoin noted the vein throbbing on Ualtar's temple and the threats swimming in his eyes. Then he looked at Muireann. She smiled weakly.

"My Queen," he began again in a rush. "I must confess I fear each measure put forth will come to nought."

The room resounded with protest, but Muireann extended her hand, bidding Eoin continue, and the wave of noise receded.

"We cannot halt the spread of this evil 'til the source of it is defeated."

Heavy was the silence that followed, for in his boyish naiveté, Eoin exposed a truth even the boldest amongst them wouldn't admit, and he, mistaking the hush for confusion, was compelled to put it to them again in plainer terms.

"So long as the Beast draws breath, we will never have peace."

Ualtar's simmering anger boiled over. "And?"

"And?" Eoin repeated with a slight stutter.

"How do *you* propose to accomplish this when legions of your betters have failed?"

"Well, I… We…"

"Go on then, boy. Spit it out. Share with us what I'm sure will be an ingenious and expertly crafted strategy."

It was painful, the disgust in his father's voice. More painful still was the disappointment Eoin saw on Muireann's face. A knife sunk into his back would have been easier to endure, but he didn't allow this to show. He lifted his chin and held fast to his conviction, no matter the cost.

"I do not know how to kill the Beast. I only know we must try while we can. When he was awake, he was hungry for the fight, yet now that he sleeps, we might have the advantage. We shouldn't waste it, small as it may be."

"Hah!" Ualtar barked out after another stretch of silence.

Thanks to this, the others found their tongues again and wagged them readily, perhaps to shame Eoin into recanting or to ease the bitter taste of cowardice. Ignoring Muireann's call for civility, they thumped on the table with closed fists and shouted out every conceivable manner of abuse.

Needles seemed to stick in Eoin's mouth. Humiliation hammered against his heart, but there was something else building inside of him, something that promised to make all of this torment worthwhile. Was it right to submit to it and give it control? He didn't care. He liked how it felt, and for once, that was enough. Somehow, he knew that the life he'd now live was vastly different than the one intended for him from birth. His words had set a new destiny into motion. He leapt to his feet, shocking the wind from his detractors' lungs.

"We've an opportunity to put an end to years of suffering, and if you won't seize it, then I will!"

Eoin stared eagerly at Muireann, willing her to understand that the opportunity he spoke of had as much to do with the stolen kisses of childhood as it did the Beast. Should he succeed, he'd become a hero such as the kingdom had not seen since ages past. And a hero like this would undoubtedly be granted many freedoms, many rewards, including perchance the hand of a woman far above his station.

"I will go, my Queen, at your command."

Yet his newfound hope, shining as it was, did not lift Muireann from the gloom into which she'd fallen. It was with regret that she gazed upon him, fixing his handsome face into her memory, because she also sensed the change of his destiny and saw with it a cruel, fruitless end. She thought of refusing him, of insisting he remain a shadow forever kept at arm's length, but as she'd broken his heart too many times already, she couldn't bear to break it again. Better to let him die while he was still revelling in the raptures of youthful idealism than to condemn him to decades of lonely despair.

"Go," she said, mustering just enough composure so as not to betray her sorrow. "Go and kill the Beast if you can, and may the grace of the gods go with you."

Thus, Eoin rode from the castle soon thereafter amidst flowers and fanfare. His smile was so bright with happiness and his cheeks so rosy with pride that no one dared tell him that he rode not to glory but certain death. Only once he disappeared into the horizon did the wailing begin. It was said Muireann wept loudest of them all, for she mourned the loss of a treasured friend as well as a life that she, as Queen, could never have. She then removed herself to her chambers, remaining sequestered there in her grief for a fortnight, and when she finally emerged, she was a changed woman, decisive, cold, and convinced that no good could ever come of love.

CHAPTER 1

After many weeks and many trials, having weathered storms put to him by nature and mankind alike, Eoin arrived at the heart of the Beast's domain. Contrary to the maps he'd studied that indicated the area was uninhabitable, he found a village there. It was a stingy, grubby, joyless place, and the sagging cluster of rain-battered buildings shoved against one another as though each swore to be the last standing.

He dismounted to lead his horse, a dependable rose-grey palfrey named Hoireabard, down the slop-covered streets. Although it was midday, the houses were quiet, the market deserted. Eoin greeted each of the few people he did happen to see, yet only the fat, glossy ravens lining the rooftops bothered to answer him. He suppressed a shudder, well aware of what had them cackling so merrily.

As the dead outnumbered the living here in the Accursed Lands, corpses were often left to rot along the roadsides. He would have liked to offer them more than prayers, but the

Beast was waiting, and unless Eoin defeated him, there would ever be more bodies than graves to hold them. He knew this. He had reminded himself of it daily during his travels.

Nevertheless, he cringed with guilt when a door banged open and two boys emerged lugging the naked body of a young man between them. It looked as if he was their brother or maybe a cousin—all three were towheaded, had receding chins, gapped teeth, and cupped ears—and he was freshly dead. He flopped into an awkward jumble when they tossed him to the gutter.

This was none of Eoin's business. He should move along. Yet he couldn't. The two boys slouched back inside, and Eoin called out to stop them.

"Surely you don't plan to…? Someone has been sent to collect him, yes?"

The taller of the two sniffed and dragged a hand beneath his filthy nose. "He's for the night."

"But—"

"For the night," said the smaller boy flatly. "That its hunger won't rip us from our beds."

Clucking his tongue, Eoin walked on. His father had always told him that one gains nought but frustration when one argues with peasants. Logic exceeds the limits of their crude intellect, and they take to superstition like a calf to a teat. It was the reason they required a ruling class, but Eoin wasn't here to rule them, and he wouldn't try to wean them off their heretical beliefs, not if they were so far gone as to treat even kin with such callous disregard.

He'd intended to lodge here for a day or two before setting out on the final leg of his journey, but that seemed unwise. Once his horse had a chance to warm his bones, Eoin would gladly leave these degenerates to their sins.

Searching out a stable, he pledged the groom a tidy sum to ensure Hoireabard received proper care then went next door to what once may have been a homely inn. Now it was as much a bog as the roads and so steeped in the sickly-sweet stench of decay that the blind would confuse it for a lich-house. The ravens must have thought likewise, for they'd staked their claim. They roosted on beams and windowsills, watching with rapt interest while Eoin ate a meal of tough, overcooked meat, watery cabbage, and mouldy bread, but there were more eyes fixed upon him than those of the birds.

Word of Eoin's arrival had spread, and the whole of the village was flocking to the inn to gawk at every part of him from every angle and view. To inspire a particular conclusion to their inspection, he kept a hand rested on the hilt of his sword. He'd nearly finished eating in this dour fashion when one of the watchers, a decrepit relic of a man, dared speak.

"Never wagered to see your kind again, Sir Knight." Without waiting for an invitation, he took a seat at Eoin's table and held out a wrinkled, leathery palm packed smooth with dirt. "Alms for the dying?"

Eoin sighed. He'd had quite enough of these people, but the toothless grin and gaunt frame did make a convincing case for charity.

"Oh, very well."

"Many thanks, Sir."

The coins had scarcely left Eoin's possession before they were swapped for ale. The old man drank his fill noisily as Eoin hurried to swallow the last few morsels of bread and push up from his chair, lest other beggars similarly abuse his goodwill.

"Going so soon?" the man asked, hiccupping. "Will you not stay a spell and talk with me?"

"No, friend, I shall not."

"*Stay*. Tell me news of other lands."

"Forgive me, but I cannot spare the time."

"What brings you to such haste?"

"The same as has brought you to such ruin."

The old man blanched. Barely managing a hiss, he said, "The Beast."

"Aye."

A flurry of whispers whirled around the inn, and then the villagers, those rough, unsavoury folk who resembled more animal than not, began to tremble and mewl.

"But why?" cried the man. "Does your life hold so little value that you would throw it away?"

"You presume the worst."

"Because I've seen the worst, Sir Knight, and I know its face as I know my own."

"And what, prithee, is its face?"

Though the old man slumped with recollection, he did not answer Eoin. His eyes unfocused, gazing out at nothing and everything, as did all other eyes in the room. No one moved or even looked to be breathing, and Eoin was suddenly struck by the notion that he stood amongst the living dead.

"Well then," he stammered. "I shall take my leave. Good day."

This roused the man from his stupor. "No! No, you mustn't! What can I say to turn you from this lunacy?" He clutched at Eoin's arm. "You remind me of my son, you see. A good man, my son. Proud. Strong. Arlyn was his name. Arlyn. My son..." And there, he lost his words and floundered to find them.

Eoin gently worked himself free of the man's grip. This had gone on long enough. Seeing the pitiful old beggar relive such a devastating loss felt too intrusive, too indecorous to stomach. He couldn't just leave the man to wallow in despair like this. It would be akin to letting the hogs at a half-dead monstrosity of a lamb without first putting it out of its misery, so Eoin gathered his full height, pulled his very best impression of his father's unflinching resolve over his face, and deepened his already deep voice.

"I promise you, friend, I will avenge Arlyn's death. On my

honour, I will kill the Beast."

He expected this would console the old man and that the rest of the villagers would applaud and cheer, but they merely sank further into themselves. They had all gone as pale, as waxen as a death mask, and the ravens above croaked as though laughing at their bloodless terror.

"Well then," Eoin repeated, yearning more than ever for escape. "I must away for now, but let us share another drink upon another day."

"I will drink to your memory, Sir Knight, as we shan't meet again."

"What pessimism!"

"What innocence," he countered, blotting milky tears with his sleeve.

"Do you truly mean for me to leave without any encouragement? Have you no blessings to give at all?"

"I won't encourage folly and my blessings are already spent. But... Since Arlyn would want it... Another danger lies before that which you so stubbornly seek. The woods sheltering the Beast's lair are cursed. Haunted. Full of treachery, godless magic, and evil spirits. I'll not speak of its horrors for risk of drawing them here, though there is one..." He crooked a boney finger to coax Eoin closer. "When you can no longer breathe for the crowding of trees, 'tis then *she* will appear to you."

"A monster?"

"A *witch*. A temptress of untold beauty, but mark me, that beauty is a lie. She is vile and merciless and cannot be trusted. Do not be deceived by her, Sir Knight, else she will be your downfall."

Then he sat back and stared sightlessly into the distant past while Eoin mulled over his warning. A Beast *and* a witch, and both hidden within what sounded to be a foe in and of itself. This wasn't the battle Eoin had anticipated, but then he'd only really thought on the result, on the prize, never so much on the details. And never on the possibility that he might fail.

Throughout his long journey, he had clung to the hope he'd known when he first set out from the castle. Now doubt crept into his heart, and as the villagers grimly raised a toast to his eternal soul and not his assured victory, Eoin was too humbled to remember what hope felt like.

He left the village eager for a lessening of pressure, a release of the invisible vice that squeezed his chest flat. No such relief occurred. He scowled. What was wrong with him?

"Death masks and laughing ravens," he muttered, twisting Hoireabard's reins in his fists until the leather creaked. "Honestly, what nonsense!"

He was acting a fool and despised himself for it. After all, he was taught better than to let his imagination run rampant like this. But imagination always *had* been the cause of Eoin's troubles, hadn't it? According to his father anyway.

"Leave the dreaming to women and the thinking to men brighter than you," he'd scold. "All you have to do is put one foot in front of the other and get on with it."

Quite right. Eoin shook his head, trying to send every last one of these uninvited ideas flying out. He didn't have to think. He had simply to fight, and thankfully, this was where his true talents lay. It was his life's purpose and the thing that would win him Muireann's love.

So let that old drunkard keep his blessings. Eoin didn't need them. And the others, those dead-eyed unfortunates still grieving their defeat, were welcome to moan and groan all they wanted. If they couldn't see Eoin for what he was, what he was capable of, then he would have to show them. Just wait. Once he defeats the Beast, he will be treated to more respect. No one will doubt his worth or dismiss him out of hand. Eoin chuckled, picturing the surprise he'll find on Ualtar's face when he returns home victorious. There. The sickness in his gut settled. His thoughts drifted to the golden future awaiting him, and he breathed a slow, cleansing sigh of contentment.

But then Hoireabard crested a hill and Eoin was dragged down to the dark place he'd only just escaped.

The woods the old man mentioned dominated the valley below. Spanning for miles with no end in sight, it thrived unnaturally in a state of decay. It was a festering sore. A greenish-black wound scratched across the earth, oozing like septic blood from dying veins. Eoin's mouth went dry. He denied himself even the smallest sip from his waterskin, considering the discomfort fitting punishment for his flighty, girlish reactions. Of course the Beast's forest wouldn't be a pretty place. That shouldn't surprise him in the least. And the view wasn't likely to improve, regardless of how long he glared at it, so best do as his father said.

One foot in front of the other.

Gritting his teeth, Eoin urged Hoireabard onwards. Hoireabard, however, refused to move.

"There, there, that's enough of that."

Eoin walked him in a tight circle then set him on course, and Hoireabard grudgingly began their descent, complaining the entire way. They followed a neglected path cut through dead, yellow grass. It made Eoin think of the grass back home, the smell of it when wet and crushed beneath his boots. He sat straighter in his saddle. His shoulders squared.

"We mustn't lose faith," he said, nodding to himself. "This is our destiny. I'm sure of it."

Despite Hoireabard's reluctance, they soon arrived at the edge of the forest. A host of gnarled elms, oaks, and alders tangled together, forming a wall, a barricade through which Eoin couldn't see, but there was an entrance. The path from the hilltop continued, although it was congested with shadow and coiling mist. It certainly did look to be haunted. Felt haunted too. Eoin never knew trees could brood, yet he suspected they were doing just that. They glowered at him, whispering to one another of his coming.

Stop it. Control yourself.

His heartbeat was so loud he nearly didn't notice what had him so upset. Then it dawned on him. It was the silence. A forest this size should be full of life, but the cheerful, busy chatter of birds and other woodland animals was absent. In its place, there was nothing. Absolutely nothing.

Hoireabard's sudden snort was an explosion of sound. He fought Eoin for control to turn back around. Part of Eoin was keen to let him.

"Steady on, son! You're all right. We'll do this together, won't we, old boy?"

The horse screamed and reared and screamed some more. Eoin's eyes flew to the trees, worrying the commotion would draw more of their sinister scrutiny. Were his father here, he would whip Hoireabard into submission. Ualtar didn't tolerate stroppy steeds or indeed stroppy men. His mercy was conditional, but Eoin's wasn't. He gave Hoireabard time to calm down and, after a fair deal of coddling, was able to lead him into the woods.

"There now. This isn't so bad, is it?"

He was lying.

If the inn was a lich-house and the villagers corpses then these woods were the netherworld itself. Neither wind nor sun penetrated the chaos of strangling boughs, and nebulous gloom seeped in from all sides once the entrance was behind them.

This made for a cautious pace. The darkness hid a labyrinth of roots, rocks, and other bothersome surprises, the most awful of which was a city's worth of shattered bone. It was everywhere. Scattered across the path. Piled at the base of each tree amongst black lichen and sweating, swollen mushrooms. There were even nests of it high in the branches above. A likeness of ice-cold water trickled down Eoin's spine. His imagination was too persuasive for his own good sometimes, but it couldn't trick him into thinking the bones merely belonged to animals.

It hadn't been the trees whispering after all. It was the ghosts of murdered peasants and merchants and knights just like him. Their rusted swords and lances lay alongside their remains as if waiting to be picked up again. Eoin threw a glance over his shoulder. There was nothing physically there, though whether through instinct or intuition, he knew beyond all doubt that he wasn't alone. If he were to close his eyes, he'd swear he was in the middle of a great hall packed with restless, addled men. Each one had a distinct presence, separate from the next. He could not see them, could not touch them, yet they were very, very real.

Skin crawling, he hoped they'd simply drift away if he paid them no mind, but he was a beacon and they were sailors lost in stormy seas. They needed to be near him. The air, already stale and sour, thinned as they pressed in close to examine him. As with the ravens in the village, he sensed desire in their curiosity, a perverse and infinite hunger.

Something thrashed in the trees to the right. Eoin readied himself for an attack, but it was only Hoireabard. His bridle had caught on a branch. Believing he was trapped, the terrified horse's last vestige of sanity snapped, and he galvanized more of the forest's ghosts with his squealing roars.

"Steady, steady on, stay put!"

Fear made Hoireabard ferocious. He couldn't recognise his master anymore. He slammed into Eoin. He kicked at him, knocked him to the ground, and would have crushed his head had Eoin not rolled out from underfoot. Bucking wildly, he broke free of the branches and then bolted as though wolves howled at his heels.

Cursing, Eoin followed the shrieking crash of hooves deep into the woods and then deeper still. In haste and in darkness, he fell more than not. His clothing tore and his hands and knees were scraped raw before he realised his mistake: Hoireabard was long gone, and Eoin had run too far from the path to find it again. Nothing looked familiar. The trees shifted every time he blinked. A tempest raged through his veins, and he freed it, shouting it to the treetops, but it returned straightaway, doubled in strength. The dead returned to him as well. As fast as he'd been, he hadn't managed to outrun them. They swirled around in a feverish, vaporous swarm, whispering and wanting, always wanting. They filled his ears with soundless noise that would deafen him if he could not make it stop.

"Come on then, you cowards!" he bellowed, brandishing his sword. "Do your worst!"

He spun this way and that, squinting at the shadows, searching for something or someone to fight. Several tense minutes passed. The stalemate drew on. And on. It wouldn't end, would it? Those who watched apparently could only watch, and Eoin could only laugh. He flung out his arm, scoffing at the useless, miserable lot of them then collapsed against the upturned roots of an enormous willow tree, too tired to think or even to care.

Oh, but he'd made a right mess of things, hadn't he? He laughed again, for what else was there to do? In a moment, he would pick himself up. He'd muddle through somehow. He always did.

That's when he heard it. The gentle lilt of a woman's voice drifted through the woods like a feather on the wind. Another ghost? Possibly, yet he didn't believe so. He picked out words and a melody too. It was a song!

> *My love is a rose,*
> *Plucked too soon from the flowerbed.*
> *My love is a jewel,*
> *That was stolen away.*
>
> *Now I sit here and weep,*
> *By the grave of my dearest love.*
> *And I'll stay here and weep,*

'til the end of my days.

Thoroughly entranced, Eoin stood and staggered towards the source, pausing now and then to listen. The space between trees increased. The gloom lifted. He scrubbed a hand over his mouth, floating with the feeling that he had awoken from a century of fay slumber, but what he found next made him wonder whether he'd actually fallen into a dream.

There was a clearing up ahead. In its centre stood a crooked little stone cottage with a mossy, thatched roof. There was a well and a garden, and there, singing to his quivering horse, was a woman of fierce beauty. She had fire in her hair and oceans in her eyes. A gilded thread of haunted sunlight danced upon her lovely face as if the sky itself sang back to her, and though she was dressed in common rags, Eoin saw at once that she was no mere beggar woman.

He had stumbled across a witch.

CHAPTER 2

or a time, Eoin and the witch took stock of each other without troubling to exchange a single word. It seemed she needn't speak at all, for her expression revealed her thoughts as they formed. Disdain was in the rise of her chin, annoyance in the pout of her ruby red lips. Curiosity played in the arch of her brow, but there wasn't even a hint of humour in her eyes, only a shrewd, calculating wit that dismissed Eoin as much as enticed him to approach.

And if he were to glance into a mirror, Eoin would find in his own face a war waging between awe and desire. He'd never seen her like. She was exquisite, blessed with the rare sort of perfection usually confined to stories and songs. Although older than him by a few years, her complexion was bright and supple, and if anything, those touches of age she did have had been placed there by the most reverential of hands to embellish her beauty, as do jewels set into a crown of gold. She was statuesque yet delicate, and her long, sleek, scarlet hair tumbled over her shoulders down to the tantalising curve of her hips. Before Eoin could stop himself, a riot of want pulled him into the clearing. The witch's cold gaze never wavered, though she did frown, which luckily brought him to his senses.

He remembered the old man's warning. Merciless, he called her. Vile. Eoin didn't doubt it. His father had taught him that nothing is as wicked as a woman who considers herself powerful, and evidently, she did. She'd an air of superiority about her and an almost masculine amount of confidence, ugly traits for a woman to possess.

Why then did his heart canter at such a ridiculous pace? Why did his skin colour as though held over hot coals? It had to be an enchantment. She was attempting to bewitch him! He stepped back, and she must have assumed he was weakening because she smirked.

The nerve!

How dare she think so highly of herself and so little of him? She was beautiful, it was true, and that may have been enough to lure any number of men into ruin, but not Eoin. He saw her for what she was. No matter how pleasing the design of its web, a spider could not be anything but a spider. Rather impressed with his insight and egged on by righteous indignation, he fixed her with every ounce of the contempt she deserved.

"The filth of your art cannot touch me," he declared,

mimicking his father's authoritative tone. "Away with you, witch."

A spark of hatred worked itself into her eyes. He had upset her, yet she waited complacently for Eoin to make good on his implied threat, and this was far more maddening than any hex she could have thrown at him.

"I said away with you! Begone from my sight!"

Smirk widening into a pearly smile, she wrapped her arms around Hoireabard's neck, and Hoireabard, the traitor, surrendered happily to her embrace.

"Have a care, shrew. You test my patience."

"Dearest little dolly," she cooed to Hoireabard. "When this silly oaf dies, please come and live with me."

Eoin's mouth hung open. He was appalled by her cheek, stung by her scorn. He tried to hide this, but the witch read him as easily as he read her. She giggled into Hoireabard's mane like a nymph rejoicing in the first blush of spring and then broke into song.

> *Red is the rush of your blood, poor boy,*
> *And white is the grind of your bone.*
> *There's not a colour inside you,*
> *That the Beast won't claim as his own.*

Unbelievable! Not only had she dragged his darkest fears into the light, but she also mocked them, made cruel sport of them. Rage crowded Eoin's head, eclipsing any semblance of self-control. A terrible impulse shook loose inside of him. His hand flexed above his sword while she tossed her hair in gleeful abandon and continued to sing.

> *He'll have the screams from your throat, poor boy,*
> *And every last tear from your eyes.*
> *But what will drop from your bowels,*
> *He'll graciously leave for the flies.*

He charged forward. Snatching her wrist, he tore her from Hoireabard and yanked her close. He glared down at her, fuming, chest heaving with bullish snorts, but then froze. What was he doing? What did he intend to do next? Eoin had never laid hands upon a woman in anger before, and despite his wounded pride, it still felt a very wrong thing to do.

However, a witch wasn't really a woman, was she? She was a servant of evil, as much of a beast as that which Eoin sought to kill, and he knew exactly what ought to be done with someone like her. He had frequently been made to play witness to it, although once had been more than enough to engrain it upon his memory. The rattling screams. The smell of burnt flesh. It was a grisly, repellent business, but that was the cost of her craft.

And yet...

As Eoin towered over her, they once again stared at each other. She neither fought nor bargained for her freedom. Limp in his grasp, the witch was sullen but accepting of his judgment. It astonished the both of them when Eoin released her.

"Forgive me. Are you...? I didn't hurt you, did I?"

She replied with the faintest of gasps. He couldn't look at her, didn't want to see her impish smile. She'd laugh again, he was sure of it, and sing another verse of her smug, sadistic song. His bluff had been called. He was too lenient, too pathetic to mete out the punishment she was due.

Aflame with embarrassment, he grabbed up Hoireabard's reins and hastened to the trees. The ghosts had better attack this time. Eoin wanted a fight. A sword in his hand would remind him of who he was. His heart may be weak, but at least his body wasn't.

One foot in front of the other and get on with it.

Yet as anxious as he was to put this humiliating encounter behind him, he couldn't help but prolong it further.

"My apologies," he muttered to the witch over his shoulder. "I shan't bother you again."

"Wait."

It wasn't so much an order as it was a question, and this persuaded him to turn around regardless of everything within him begging against it. Remarkably, she was changed. Softened. Where there had been arrogance, there was uneasiness, concern where there'd been disgust. She'd lost the haughty splendour of a rose and gained the humble sweetness of heather.

"Night will soon be here," she said in a clumsy, halting manner.

"What of it?"

Refusing to meet his eyes, she looked instead at Hoireabard, at the trees, the sky, the dirt beneath her bare feet. Eoin watched in fascination as she argued with herself. Finally, with apparent effort, she tugged the words from her throat.

"By day, these woods are dangerous. By night, they are deadly. Y-you'd best stay 'til morning."

Eoin blinked. Half a minute of stunned silence passed. Then he burst out laughing.

"You are clever, witch, but not so clever as you think."

"The same can be said for you," she threw back at him, instantly slipping into a scowl that could wither fruit on the vine. "I'm offering a kindness I don't give to many, though you obviously don't deserve it. Sleep in my garden and live. Or leave and die."

Eoin laughed harder. She sputtered and seethed, impotent against his amusement. When she'd had her fill of it, which didn't take long, she stomped into her cottage. There wasn't a door to close, merely a ragged curtain of deerskin, and she flung this aside with such force that it fluttered to the ground. Eoin's sides nearly split.

He toyed with the idea of teasing her a tad more, but as she said, the night was on its way. He needed a place to make camp, and it seemed safer out there with the ghosts and the gloom than here with her. Thus, Eoin called out his farewell. Poor spider. Her web was spun with skill, yet she'd have to go without supper tonight.

Dragging Hoireabard along, Eoin left the witch's yard. The trees here were younger, smaller, rising in odd angles from the otherwise barren earth. Since little else grew, the meandering trail was easy to follow, and although the lack of undergrowth allowed for an unhindered view of the bones strewn about, they'd become a common sight and, like all things familiar, lost their previous menace. The lingering dead were also less threatening than before. They did remain keen on stalking his step but didn't whisper or swarm. Eoin wondered at the difference in them, ultimately deciding that it must be because of the difference in him.

And he had the pretty wee witch to thank for it.

She was a test. The gods set her in his path to distract him from destiny, but he had outfoxed her. Moreover, though she'd tried her hardest to break his spirits, the witch actually repaired them. His faith was restored, his courage refreshed. Whatever came next, Eoin was ready for it.

Perhaps after he killed the Beast, he should pay her another visit. She deserved to be made aware of how helpful she'd been to him, and he would very much like to see that fine face twist up in temper again. In fact, he found the prospect so agreeable he directed all thought towards it, preferring this fancy even over the one in which he returned to Muireann.

What would she sing then? Would she still dare to call him a silly oaf? He cracked a grin. No. She would have to admit that she, like the villagers, had underestimated him. She would bow to him and plead for mercy and forgiveness. Eoin would grant both, of course, as he was a generous man. The wicked ice in her veins would thaw, she'd promise to reform, and he would be celebrated all the more for conquering not only a beast but a strange and savage beauty.

Engrossed in these lively musings, Eoin walked on through the woods, neglecting to notice the day's end until a waxing sliver of moon sailed above him. He also didn't notice when the ghosts' lidless eyes widened in anticipation and something new, something corporeal and profane and sharp of tooth, joined in their pursuit.

CHAPTER 3

I t is a nasty thing to wake from the pleasures of reverie, to fall from soaring heights of imagination. It's far nastier still to be cast out of a beautiful dreamscape and crash straight into a nightmare. Thus it was for Eoin, who in one moment was lost amongst the clouds and in the next was surrounded by a frenzied horde of hellions.

He couldn't guess their numbers. Some were the size of badgers, others huge as the mightiest of hounds, but even the largest amongst them sped through the night swift as wind. They ran at him on four legs and then on two, grunting and squealing and howling. Eoin hadn't time to collect his wits or reach for his sword. His arms flew up to cover his head as they attacked with tooth and claw. A crimson mist sprayed into the air. He knew it was his blood but, in his panic, could not yet feel the wounds.

Beside him, Hoireabard careened back and forth, bellowing

in terror. The creatures hooted while they slashed open his flank, and it was laughter, Eoin realised. It was joy. They dragged the horse down. His final trumpeting cries made Eoin scream too. He heard his own murder in those shrieks, felt the frigid kiss of death press against his lips.

It wasn't enough to shield himself. He had to fight. He punched them, stomped on them, bashed them against trees. Nothing shook them off for long. They kept coming back for more. He flung out his hands to tear at the fiend in front of him, but its hide was unyielding, thicker than the best of armour, and Eoin's nails peeled from their beds. In desperation, he struggled on, eventually ferreting out a weakness. Under the arms, running from wrist to waist was a stunted, parchment-thin set of wings. Eoin ripped them into shreds, and the devil retreated to the darkness, yelping as it went.

Another hurled itself at Eoin's face. This one was smaller but as furious as a feral cat. As Eoin held it at bay, their eyes locked together, and for an instant, he saw what resembled human emotion. A hideous, crazed emotion, though human nonetheless.

What a loathsome discovery, finding such eyes glaring out from behind the muzzle of a monster. They were the brush of an unseen hand in an empty room, the thud from beneath the bed when all else is quiet. Eoin couldn't stand to look at them. Could not suffer their very existence. He fought past champing teeth to plunge his thumbs into them, and when they burst, he shuddered with satisfaction. Blinded, gurgling miserably, the creature bounded away.

"Who's next?!" Eoin shouted to the others.

He beat his chest with his fist and then he roared, taunting them, but even though the setting sun rebels with a brilliant spectacle of colour, the night invariably triumphs. Eoin was stumbling. He was dizzy from loss of blood, too dizzy. The strength he had left drained like water through a sieve. *I'm going to die*, he thought, and this thought was a question with which his mutilated body agreed. He would fall as Hoireabard had, with tongue protruding and limbs splayed. With his organs exposed and the steaming loops of his entrails spilling out. And these freaks, these abominations, would feed off him. They'd crack his bones to suck the marrow, and afterwards, when all trace of him was gone, they would remember his taste with a smile.

So, he unsheathed his sword, raised it in defiance, and roared again, releasing his disappointment, fear, and the squandered potential of his youth.

Though the creatures closest to him quailed, another looked up from where it was busying itself with Hoireabard's carcass. It was a tremendous brute, the biggest yet, with fully formed wings in place of arms. The stack of muscles making up its long throat rolled and rippled as it growled in answer to Eoin's challenge.

They met in a violent clash, but Eoin's sword, although forged by the finest bladesmiths and unfailing in past battles, proved as useless as his hands against the rock-like flesh of his enemy. It was a mere matter of seconds before the creature sunk finger-length fangs into Eoin's shoulder. With ease, it jerked him off his feet, thrashed him side to side, and threw him down.

It waited, leering while Eoin crawled to his knees, its ghastly eyes again too human, too cunning. Just as Eoin was about to stand, it pounced on him and pressed him into the mud. Curdling gore dripped from its wolfish maw onto Eoin's neck. The fight was over. He had lost.

"Do it then," he commanded in a whisper.

The others danced around, whistling and clacking, eager for the finish, rabid for the feast. Eoin tried to block it out, wishing his last thoughts to be of Muireann, but the noise of their victory was too awful to ignore.

Then a scream cut through all other sound.

The witch!

Moonlight dazzled against her skin and blazed in her flowing red hair, and truly, she was a goddess descended from on high. Eoin flooded with heat. So lovely! It must have been a vision, a winsome figment of his dying mind, and though he knew not why she stood in place of his Queen, he was glad to see her.

"Stop!" she said. "Please stop!"

Contorting its already grotesque face into a grimace of rage, the creature climbed off Eoin and slithered towards her. Eoin sucked in a breath of cold shock. This was no illusion. She was really there, alone and defenceless amongst a pack of marauding devils, and witch or no, he couldn't let them hurt her.

"Leave her!" he cried, groping for his sword. Blood bubbled in his mouth and through the choking, he yelled, "Take me!"

No such luck. It was the witch they wanted now. Despairing, he prayed to any god who might be listening to grant him the power to secure her escape, but gods are fickle, indifferent at the best of times, deliberately cruel at the worst, and his prayers went unanswered. He collapsed. The monsters were as shapeless phantoms, darting about too fast for his weary eyes to follow. He could only wait, heartsick with grief and self-disgust, for the witch's scream to rise above their horrid yowls once more.

But if it did, it was beyond Eoin's awareness. The world blurred then faded to black, and he tumbled into an abyss that reached up to catch him. Before consciousness slipped away into nothingness, he felt a soft, warm hand cup his cheek. Someone murmured that everything was going to be all right in a voice so achingly earnest that he could almost believe them. He chuckled. In death, his wayward imagination had finally been put to good use.

CHAPTER 4

E oin did not die, although for a long while, nothing could convince him he hadn't. Time swelled and shrank, sped forward and doubled back. He sat on his old nurse's knee, sucking a rag dipped in honey and milk. He writhed on a lumpy bed, shivering with sweat and begging for release. Muireann arrived. She was a portrait on the wall that sprang to life when he groaned her name. Arms above her head, she leapt and twirled, spinning faster, glowing brighter, transforming into a flame flickering on a candle's wick.

As he cried out for the loss of her, he was caressed by those same clever hands that had comforted him before. They glided across him gently, so very gently, lighting upon his pulse like the daintiest of butterflies. If not a butterfly then like a fairy, for the accompanying voice charmed his attention away from the invisible crowd that babbled incessantly in his ears. The fairy and her hands became Eoin's religion. He mumbled devotions to her whenever she tipped water onto his shrivelled tongue. He clung to her and whimpered, terrified she would forsake him as had all other gods.

And so he existed in this wretched state, more child than man, more dead than alive, until his fever broke and the fairy's lullaby coaxed him into deep, undisturbed dreams. When next he woke, time moved along its proper course. Muireann no longer teased him from atop the candles, and he discovered that what he worshipped wasn't goddess or fairy but a witch.

Peering through cracked eyelids, Eoin watched as she hovered over him, humming to herself whilst washing him with a wet cloth. There was no part of his body she didn't bathe, but he was too sore for modesty, and she was too absorbed in her work to spot that he was awake. He was able to observe her at his leisure and was again astonished by just how pretty she was—so strangely, otherworldly pretty—that he felt driven to find even one single flaw. There was a blotch of green just above the sun-kissed apple of her cheek, yet this was plainly a fading bruise, and similarly, the faint wrinkle pinching into the ripened berry richness of her lips was just an old scar. Neither of these nor the almost grandmotherly frown of concentration she wore was anywhere near to being a genuine flaw. Her beauty, therefore, was essentially irreproachable.

Irritated by this conclusion, Eoin looked past the witch to the deer hide in the doorway then around the rest of the room. Much better. He saw plenty for his spite to pick apart. Her cottage was a hovel. It was drafty, cramped, and bleak. What furniture she possessed was better suited for kindling and had none of the whimsical embellishments that women typically delight in adding. Even the bundles of herbs she'd hung up to dry were dreary, every one a muddy shade of brown, nothing at all like the colourful array in the storehouses and apothecaries of home. Pathetic. That was the only word that came to Eoin as he took in his surroundings. It was a word often thrown about by gossiping courtiers who would passionately pretend they'd said it in sympathy if the wrong person happened to overhear them. Eoin didn't have to pretend. Although he wanted something to hold over the witch, he couldn't content himself with faults born of poverty and was instead gripped by melancholy. How odd. Why should he care that a witch lived in squalor? He blew out a befuddled sigh.

Immediately, the witch's hands were snatched from his skin. He turned to her. She stared back, her blue-grey eyes growing owlish in size. As before, they spoke to each other without speaking, but the fever had dulled Eoin's senses, boiled them until his thoughts were treacle-thick. He couldn't keep up with the conversation. It hurt him to try, though try he must. His life might well depend on it.

Yet the witch was just as contrary as ever and purposefully averted her gaze, rearranged his blankets, and then bustled to the fire pit where a small, dented iron pot warmed over smouldering embers.

She started to talk but only squeaked. Once she'd chased the mouse out of her throat by coughing into her fist, she asked, "Hungry?"

He was, surprisingly. The thin broth she gave him might as well have been ambrosia. Eoin moaned in bliss. His stomach rumbled, demanding more. She couldn't spoon it out fast enough to appease his appetite, so he grabbed the bowl.

"Mind yourself."

He ignored her. He shouldn't have. Spasms sliced through his arms like red-hot blades, and he flopped down, wheezing and wincing.

"Greedy boy!" she exclaimed, waggling a pointed finger in time with three sharp clicks of her tongue. "Serves you right."

If Eoin had not been in such agony, her impertinence would have angered him, but he excused it away because she had begun to stroke through his hair. Her light, tickling touch and the soft shushing noises she made eventually relieved enough of his pain that he could breathe again. After this, they formed a truce of sorts. She fed him, washed him, redressed his wounds, and rubbed new life into dying muscle. In return, Eoin didn't resist. Even when she forgot her place, which was more often than not, and ordered him about, he allowed her to care for him without interference, without independence, lest he thwart his recovery and waste her efforts.

But all the while, he had to wonder: Why? Why did she help him? She was a witch. She was, by nature, irredeemably evil. Evil did not cure what it could simply let die. It had none of the compassion, patience, or generosity that she seemed to have. What did that mean? Was it a ploy? To what end? He studied her face again and again, but although it continued to be a revelation of emotion, he just couldn't fit the disparate pieces of her personality together as a whole.

She was kind yet aloof. Selfless yet severe. Hot-tempered as a wild boar with the attentiveness of a mother hen. She moved about the cottage with the lithe, willowy step of a highborn lady yet otherwise had a scandalous lack of social graces. When exhaustion nudged Eoin into less cautious and more charitable moods, he would concede that, given her isolation, most of her shortcomings were understandable. Recluses did tend to have very different ideas as to what constituted proper behaviour compared to the rest of society. Though irksome, off-putting, and erratic, they were harmless eccentrics generally, and had Eoin not known that she was a witch, he might have thought her harmless too.

But he *did* know.

He scowled at the roof. Of all things to divide his resolve, his opinion of a witch should certainly not be one of them. His father wouldn't be won over by her, no matter how comely she was nor how healing her hands. He'd kill her at his first opportunity. Eoin would probably be wise to do the same, but as he hadn't the nerve to kill her before, what made him think he could do so now? And even assuming he could, how was it in any way honourable to put her to death without taking everything she'd done for him into account?

Days crawled by in a haze as Eoin amassed a collection of unanswerable questions, and soon their burden became too unruly to manage. It was time for a more direct approach. To learn what the witch had planned for him, to peel the truth apart from what he feared was a façade, he'd have to earn her trust. A daunting task. Charm didn't come as instinctively to Eoin as it did to other men. He hadn't the vaguest notion where to begin.

One foot in front of the other...

He asked for water. After he drank his fill, he thanked her, but he must have said it too softly, for she turned away without so much as a nod. He tried a bit louder. She awkwardly stoked an already healthy fire and refused to acknowledge him even when he repeated himself for the third time.

Eoin bristled. "Don't act as though you don't hear me, witch."

Her half-hearted, fumbling jabs at the fire suddenly became deliberate strikes. "Witch," she muttered as though to an audience that did not include Eoin. "In another life, I had another name, yet in this one, I'm only called Witch."

"Oh, so your ears *do* work?"

"Better than your tongue at any rate," she grumbled.

"Meaning?"

"That it ought not to insult the one who saved you from

death."

"You—" He took a moment to compose himself. Restraint was more important than ever, especially since antagonizing her would damage his designs to win her over. "You're right. I'm sorry that I offended you. What would you rather I call you?"

She copied him, pausing just as he had, but not for the same reason. Angling her head to catch a more flattering light, she preened a bit and smiled at Eoin seductively. "*Witch*," she breathed in an airy whisper then sneered with contempt as she stabbed a hellish cascade of sparks from the flames.

He could have screamed. She was impossible! Insufferable! Eoin may have been a more tolerant man than most, but even he had limits and somehow she could bring him to them in an instant. His hands curled into claws and then fists, and he cursed her for her stubborn pride before the cramping in his arms forced him to abandon the defence of his own.

Stay focused, Eoin. Don't stoop to her level. This pettiness is beneath you.

However, while he lay there waiting for the flood of outrage to recede, his mind kept wandering towards the most peculiar of places. It was a thought so foreign to him that it demanded immediate exploration. Eoin normally hadn't any use for quarrelling, and he could never fathom why some people seemed quite so fond of it, but now it was starting to make sense. He left every clash he had with the witch feeling a little more alive than he had before. He wouldn't say that he was pleased by this, yet there was no use denying it.

Still standing at the fire, the witch huffed. She'd seen the smirk on his face and clearly didn't approve of it. Fair enough. He didn't like it when she smirked either.

Or did he?

"I swear, you must be the most vexing woman to ever walk the earth," he said to her on an uncharacteristically mischievous whim. "And I'm a knight, you know, so I won't swear to something unless I mean it."

"Bully for you. But do please tell me, oh Great Sir Knight, would you prefer that I curtsey or that I bow whenever I go outside to empty your chamber pot?"

Although this sarcastic piece of bait was truly tempting, Eoin declined to take a bite because he had a theory he wanted to test. The witch glared at him and then at the flames, poking them as though to get the reaction she wasn't getting from him any longer. At last, she stopped harassing the fire to perch upon a rickety chair, and for the next few minutes, she snuck furtive glances at Eoin while growing ever more frustrated that he wasn't offering further excuses to abuse him.

"Let's not fight. We can at least be civil, can't we?" Eoin asked, again gauging her response.

"I can," she replied as she eagerly turned up her nose. "Not so sure about you, though. I've never known men to concern themselves much with civility."

"Well, you've never known me."

She scoffed. "And I don't want to."

"I've a hunch you haven't the choice, as I'll be reliant on your hospitality for some time to come."

"We won't talk."

"No?"

"There's no need."

"But what if I want to thank you again? You have, as mentioned, saved my life."

Sulking, she fidgeted in her chair while a grin tickled the corners of Eoin's mouth. She was such a queer little miss, rude and unrepentant, yet there was no doubt that she was enjoying their banter just as much as he was. A blush had swept up her cheeks, far too bright to have been only a trick of the firelight.

"Tell me your name," he said when she looked over and caught him staring.

"Why?" she asked suspiciously.

"Because friends generally refer to each other by name."

Something flashed across her eyes. Like a bolt of lightning, it charged the space between them so that it crackled with pressure, but she promptly blinked it away.

"We aren't friends."

"We could be."

She scoffed again, albeit shakily. "Tedious man. Go to sleep, won't you?"

Eoin was too intrigued to be deterred, and although a

bonfire built in his wounds, he sat up. The effort, excruciating as it was, worked as he'd hoped. Fussing and fretting, she hastened to his side to case him back down. Now was his chance. He clasped his fingers loosely around her wrist. There! Another flash of that strange light.

"You're frightened."

"I am not." The way she yanked free insisted otherwise.

He tried once more to get up. His body increased its resistance, and as it screeched out a list of grievances, the room lurched then spun. Eyes squeezed shut, teeth bared and clenched, Eoin marshalled enough breath to speak without retching. "I don't understand. Why are you afraid of me now, when I'm so completely at your mercy? You weren't the least bit afraid before."

She didn't reply, but he heard tightness in her throat as she swallowed, which seemed an answer in itself. He peeked at her and saw that her fear had taken new form. Pain. Though it was of a different variety than Eoin's, it was equally paralysing. She wasn't able to control her face, to sharpen it to a knife's point as was her custom. She wasn't even able to look away. Neither was Eoin. They were suddenly trapped together in a patch of time filled with urgency and secrets and longing, all unspoken but all shared. The sensation, the sheer intimacy of it, was more than Eoin could stand.

"Forgive me," he blurted out.

Apparently as uncomfortable as Eoin, she started braiding

her hair in a very gruff yet very disordered fashion. "Whatever for?"

"I…I don't know. For everything, I suppose."

His father would beat him for this and perhaps, once he was healed, Eoin would regret it, but that was a worry for another day. Maybe trust could only be received once it was given, and even though she was a witch, she was also the woman who doted on him so tirelessly, who'd offered him sanctuary even after he had threatened her, who'd sung so sweetly to calm poor old Hoireabard before she had ever known anything of Eoin's existence. And if that woman was suffering, Eoin was to blame. He had been the instigator of their little war after all. Any barbs she'd flung at him had been in retaliation for those he'd thrown first.

"We can begin again," he said, shame twisting a corkscrew into his chest. "Let's pretend we've only just met."

"Don't be ridiculous."

"Why not? I'm good at it, aren't I?"

She bit her lip to hide a smile.

"I'll take that as a 'yes,' which means we have one thing in common. We both think I'm a fool."

She had a choice then. To allow the smile to show or draw blood trying to kill it. After exchanging a glance with Eoin, she chose the former. She was on the verge of flustered laughter, as was he, and it stopped the corkscrew from turning.

"You may call me Fool if you'd like. Or Tedious. Or

Greedy or even Silly Oaf." He held out his hand. "But for what it's worth, I'm Eoin."

She stared as if bewildered. Eventually, just before his arm lost strength, she took his hand in hers. There was a tremble in it, wet heat in its palm, ice in its fingertips. He squeezed it experimentally. Once again, she yanked herself free, and once again, she fixated on her braid.

"You said as much," she mumbled to the fire. "When you were sick."

"Did I?"

She nodded.

"What else did I say?"

"Nonsense mostly." Her mouth wobbled open then pressed shut, and then she said, "Cinnia."

"I beg your pardon?"

"My name is Cinnia."

"Tell me a story."

"*Another* one?"

He tried to feign annoyance but failed miserably, and she gave his hair a friendly tousle before pulling her chair next to the bed. It was a small gesture, seemingly insignificant, yet it filled Eoin with pride because that chair and the drag marks it left on the dirt floor were proof of their blossoming rapport. Each passing day saw that chair inch closer and closer to him. They whiled away many an hour with Cinnia sat upon it, one knee drawn against her chest, listening intently to anything Eoin thought to share.

"Please," she said, her lips falling into a charming pout. "I want to hear about your home again."

"It isn't as though there's been a change since I last told you of it."

"But you left out the best parts!"

Eoin chuckled. She had such a clever, curious mind, one so starved by the sameness of her reclusive life that it had grown too ravenous, too impatient to be constrained by the trappings of etiquette. He routinely woke to find her waiting, ready to bombard him with questions from the second he opened his eyes, and she hounded him to expand on each explanation, to describe everything down to the tiniest detail, even those he considered irrelevant. She wanted watery-green vistas seen from mist-drizzled mountaintops, an ardent chorus of frogs on a lazy summer's night, and the fragrant, golden cosiness of freshly baked bread. That Eoin hadn't paid more attention to the pretty little particulars of his homeland completely baffled her. It baffled him too now that he longed for all he'd taken for granted, thus he obliged Cinnia as best he could. However, as it felt rather odd for a man to witter away about such frippery as birdsong, he decided he must toy with her first to help lessen his inhibitions.

"I'm sure I don't know what you mean," he said in a sly voice.

"Ah, but you are a mulish man."

"And you a mulish woman."

They glared at each other playfully. It was in moments like this that he found her most beautiful, although it had nought to do with her figure or her face. Even if she were a shrivelled old crone, he'd think the same. When her guard dropped, when she gave a glimpse of what lay beneath the witch, she shone as the spirits who dance in northern skies, and Eoin basked in her glow.

Ideas he had never braved to say aloud flowed out as freely as though he'd cracked a wax seal and read from a letter that had been folded up inside of him for years. He talked of trees as if they were temples, dragonflies as if they were fairy steeds. His poetry was admittedly crude and hastily cobbled together, but Cinnia did not mind. Enraptured, she hung on his every word, sighing, giggling now and then, and when Eoin described the plummy haze of a field of flowering spring squill, she wriggled in puppy-like pleasure.

"I remember those!" she exclaimed. "There were heaps of them growing in the meadow just outside town. They were my mother's favourite, and I..."

Blanching, without explanation or apology, Cinnia dragged her chair back over to her flimsy table and took up the work she had earlier set down—plucking the remains of a spider's banquet from a mass of cobwebs—with renewed vigour. Though the squat clay pot in which the cleaned webs were stored was empty, there really was no rush to refill it. Excluding the deepest gashes on his shoulder, Eoin's arms no longer needed to be packed and the threat of his bleeding to death had passed. He could move without reopening the wounds, and he did so, sitting up, swinging his legs over the side of the bed.

"What's wrong?"

She answered with a shrug. She'd gone stiff all over, as wooden as the table, but he knew how to soften her again.

"Cinnia," he called, for there was nothing she appeared to relish more than the sound of her own name.

Success! She returned his rueful smile.

"I haven't upset you, have I?"

"No. No, of course not. Forgive me, Eoin. I am unused to this."

"This?"

"Conversation. Company." She held out a tuft of webbing. "Spiders are not known for their wit."

They laughed together, but a nettle-like prick from his conscience reminded Eoin that it wasn't so long ago that he thought her to be a spider herself. How dreadfully ignorant of him. How peevish and unfair. She was not a spider but a cat whose tail had been stepped on once too often, shy and skittish, sniffing for danger, flinching as if expecting blows that obviously never came. The cold confidence she presented to Eoin at first was but a mask, and luckily for them both, he'd seen through it. It was gentle handling she needed, so he was patient, he was polite, and she responded to this modest civility with an almost fanatical degree of enthusiasm, much like a little flockless hatchling imprinting itself upon whomever it can. Such unconditional approval was a rare gift, one that deserved an equal return.

"You're doing fine," he said. "Believe me, your wit is far more engaging than most."

"Liar."

"I never lie."

"Hmm, I could almost believe that, were you not such an awful tease."

"I'm not! Or at least, not usually. Something about you just brings it out of me."

"…Is that so." Clipped words and a poorly concealed wince. She'd taken an insult he hadn't meant to give.

"Oh no, please don't mistake me! That was a compliment! A way of telling you that you… That I…" He gave up with a sigh. "I must confess that I'm not known for my wit either. The truth is I am nearly as unused to conversation as you."

Scepticism scribbled over the hurt on her face. "But you're a nobleman."

"Yes."

"Well, aren't there plenty of people about for you to boss around?"

"I don't 'boss around' anyone," Eoin replied, inwardly

grinning at her choice of words. "I either take or relay orders."

She tossed her hand as though he'd just proven her right.

"That's not the same as conversation, and you know it, Cinnia."

"Then what about the friends you have?" she persisted. "And your family? Surely you talk all the time with them."

"They talk. I listen."

"Why?"

"Because this is the way things are done."

"But why?"

She asked this so matter-of-factly, so innocently perplexed, that it took Eoin aback. Did she honestly have such little awareness of the world outside her forest?

"I was taught that there are certain expectations," he said as he gathered his thoughts up from the mess they'd become. "Conventions, if you will, which must be followed."

"Conventions?"

"Yes."

"Which prevent you from speaking?"

"Not speaking, per se, but…"

How could he best explain it? He wanted to say that after a lifetime spent biting his tongue, it was a welcome change to feel so free in the presence of another, to be as merry or as maudlin as he chose without fear of reproach, yet this wasn't actually the case, was it? It couldn't be, not while she kept her own tongue so firmly clamped between her teeth. If she would only just give him more of an idea of where her invisible wounds lay, he could avoid them, but although Cinnia had quickly come to uncover every last little thing about him, she'd yet to reveal that much about herself. Time and again, she sang to avoid the questions Eoin asked of her.

He ought to have been annoyed by this. Suspicion should have nagged at him like a harried, unloved wife until he did something about it. He meant to. Honestly, he did. Each time she sidestepped him with a song, he swore to stand firm, but the celestial heights her voice achieved were so captivating that it seemed more of a reward than anything else, and as he didn't wish to pry or push her too far too fast, he let the matter rest. Only in the most shadowy corner of the most secret chamber of his heart would he admit that he now dreaded what there was to learn about her. One misspoken word or even the slightest hint of darkness sprinkled into her light could potentially obliterate the trust they'd built. He couldn't risk that. Not while he was still so unwell. More to the point, he didn't want to. He liked her, liked being with her too much to go snooping around for something that might put an end to his fun.

While he mused over this for what was perhaps the hundredth time, Cinnia quietly watched him. She was reading him, Eoin assumed, and receiving what further explanation she required from the involuntary movements of his lips, jaw, and brow. That they could communicate so well without words was proving to be both a blessing and a curse. He felt so exposed under her scrutinous gaze that he squirmed. Thankfully, she turned her concentration to her uplifted hand where she rubbed the sticky residue from the cobwebs between finger and thumb.

"I believe I understand," she began with the slow, methodical enunciation of a philosopher. "You speak, but you don't truly talk. You don't express what's in your heart because you know, as I do, that there are some things better left unsaid. They are like flowers. Flowers will never be so lovely as they are in the instant before they've been picked. That's what my mother used to say anyway." Her eyes snapped back to Eoin's. "Do you love your mother?"

Of all questions to ask! And without any warning. Eoin broke into laughter that hitched and pitched in near maniacal confusion.

"Well? Do you?"

"Why, yes," he stuttered. "Yes, of course."

"Do you really? Or do you only just respect her? Because there is a difference." He didn't have an opportunity to answer because she hurriedly added, "I loved mine. Adored her. She's dead now, though. Long dead."

Eoin sobered at once. "I'm so sorry."

He reached his arms towards her. It was such a natural response, to offer comfort just as she'd done when he was sick or suffering through nightmares of the attack. Cinnia did not, however, even acknowledge his offer. As though yanked to her feet by invisible strings, she carried the pot of webbing over to her cupboard and set it down with brusque but muted precision. Then she devoted herself to idle tasks, straightening what was already straight, brushing away dust that had yet to settle.

"All for the best," she said, and this artifice of indifference might have been convincing were it not for the story narrated by her face. "My mother wasn't like me. She'd have gone mad with... Without the spring squill." She licked her lips. "Never mind. What's done is done. She's been in my dreams lately, that's all."

Eoin waited. Said nothing. Did nothing. There was an elemental force at work here, one that would not be denied. It was dredging up what Cinnia had tried to drown, and if she needed time to sort through the wreckage, then it was Eoin's privilege to provide it. He reached towards her again, not with his arms but his eyes, and in a silence more sacred than any he'd ever known, he became the vessel into which she could pour her grief. This new offer was accepted. Eoin saw the relief that it gave her ripple across her skin. She sucked in a laugh as though she didn't quite believe this could be real or that it could last, but the longer it did, the more she wanted. The invisible puppeteer took charge of her again, and she was brought over to Eoin in awkward, tentative steps. Then all at once, the strings were cut. She tumbled down beside him, sweet breath tickling his ear as she leaned against him on the bed. His injured shoulder screamed as it strained under her weight, yet he didn't care.

"So stupid of me," she said between wet sighs. "I don't even remember what she looked like."

"Then tell me what you do remember."

"Her smile. Her tenderness. I felt safe with her. Protected. I think I miss that feeling more than I actually miss her." She gasped and pulled away from him. "Does that sound horrible?"

"No, Cinnia, not at all. It makes perfect sense."

Soothed for the moment, she rested her forehead against his chin. "I wish I could go back. Be a child with a mother again. I was happy then. I was myself. I don't know who I am now. There's been a stranger living in me for so long, I can't get rid of her. Even if I could shed my skin, she'll still be there, raw and red, and we will harden together into the wrong shape once more. But if I could somehow go back, change things…"

"You could hide from the stranger," he finished for her, dizzied by warmth in his veins that did not stem from the stubbornly lingering effects of fever. "You could be happy."

She looked up at him, eyes gone soft and starry, and nodded.

Life was an uncharted, snaking road. Every bend in it, every turn and fork, had led Eoin to these woods and to this cottage where he had discovered, in the most implausible circumstances, a friend. A true friend. Perhaps even a lifelong one. Her first confession, if that's what it was, hadn't destroyed trust but deepened it, and surely trust such as that had the power to change one's path, to right old wrongs, and absolve the sins of even the most wicked of witches.

Nevertheless, though it might indeed be that powerful, trust was also impossibly fragile and lost much more quickly than can be gained.

When Eoin awoke late that night, he found a dying fire and a room that felt stripped bare because Cinnia was not there to distract from its ugliness. He called out her name to no avail. He waited and slept some more, but when he woke again, she still hadn't returned. A wee mouse of worry began to nibble away inside of him, and although his legs were clumsy from lack of use, he got up to go out in search of her.

And immediately wished he hadn't.

The sky was hung with corpse lights, pale balls of wispy blue flame said to be omens of death. The shuffling forest was hung with eyes. And teeth. Though there was no doubt they still thought him prey, the creatures didn't move with predatory stealth this time. They wanted Eoin to know they were there, that they were waiting for him, that night after night, they whetted their appetites with his smell and watered Cinnia's garden with drops of their drool, and they wanted him to know all this because it wasn't just his flesh they were after but his fear.

Pride ordered him to deny them this at least, yet the animal within begged him to run. Run! Away from these woods and the unclean things they sheltered. But he couldn't run, nor could he fight. Not with this crippled body and these empty hands. Hide then, cried the panicked animal, and Eoin scurried backwards into the cottage.

Walls of shifting, crumbling stone. No door to speak of. How had he ever slept in here, felt safe in here? Whatever glamour had been cast on him had obviously worn itself out, for he was once again seeing with clear eyes. But it was too late. Much too late. He heard the snap of branches followed by the soft, dull thudding of several feet hitting the ground. Paws padded towards the door. Claws clicked against stray pebbles in the yard.

Then he heard *her*.

"What do you think you're doing?" Cinnia asked of the monsters hunting him in a whisper too unruffled to have any qualms of being hunted herself.

During the weeks spent in her care, although he often amused himself imagining just how she managed to save him from them, Eoin had never found the right time to ask her what had happened. Instead, he'd pictured cryptic words shouted to the heavens above, fire and lightning forged into swords, and even an unending supply of soldiers conjured from the mud, but no. Evidently, there hadn't been a battle, of any kind, at all.

"Get away from there," she said with less bother than it

took to shoo a fly. "Oh, don't give me that look. He belongs to me, remember? You promised."

The creatures snarled and whined, but it sounded as though she was successfully herding them back into the trees.

"Quickly now. Go on. Shhh! Don't wake him. Make for the village if you're so hungry. I'm sure something's been left out for you to eat."

Children in play are oblivious to the oily black leeches that lurk in the shallows until the revolting things have grown fat on their blood. They cannot see how badly they've dirtied their clothes until their cheeks sting with the impression of an adult's hand. A child's world is shrunk down and sanitized into the best possible version of itself, and that is exactly what Eoin had done to the world he'd been sharing with Cinnia. But their indulgent little game of make-believe ended the instant she drew aside the deerskin curtain and finally noticed that Eoin had heard what he could never pretend away.

CHAPTER 5

hen he was small, just an apple-cheeked lad with a quick laugh and a lively step, his father announced that Eoin would soon be sent away to further the training they'd begun. Eoin beamed with pride. This was an honour, a long-awaited rite of passage. He talked of little else and lost sleep every night dreaming of the many daring adventures he'd have. However, on the morning he was to leave, after he exchanged farewells with his family and was sat atop a shy, twitching pony, he had an abrupt change of heart. Crying like a babe, he threw himself on the ground.

"I don't wanna go! Please, can I stay?"

This did nothing to ingratiate Eoin to Ualtar, who had never been the most solicitous of fathers. He took his embarrassment of a son to task, but no amount of punishment liberally applied to his bottom induced Eoin to get back up on that pony.

"Let the boy alone," said his mother, Bronagh, suddenly.

As she rarely spoke above a whisper, her forceful demand gave all who heard it a shock. She held out her hand. Eoin hesitated, looking to his father for approval.

"Come," she insisted.

He slipped his hand into hers. It was an odd sensation. Whilst cordial to him as most women are to children, his mother wasn't particularly affectionate. In fact, he learned fairly young that, as a general rule, she didn't want to be touched. A pat on the head was the most he could expect from her, and when the little day-to-day injuries of boyhood caused him distress, he was more likely to seek out Nurse or even Cook than the one who'd given him life.

Together, they walked beyond the stables, past the manor house, and through a field of tall grass glistening with dew. As they crushed the grass beneath their feet, a sweet green smell rose into the air. Whenever Eoin recalled this day, he could summon that very scent and with it came the rush of emotion, the fear and the sadness and the strangeness of it all.

He was brought to the lone hawthorn presiding over the furthest corner of the field. Cradled in its roots was a gurgling spring of cold, clear water, and in the spring, there lived a Spirit, benevolent when shown respect, wrathful when offended, so they searched about their persons for suitable gifts. His mother pulled a silver pin from her hair and placed it into the water. Eoin hadn't anything to offer, but Bronagh passed him a coin, which he carefully drove into the hawthorn's trunk with a piece of stone.

"This is a test," she then said to him. "The first of many that life will put to you. You cannot hide from these tests, for their results are what will shape you into a man. Don't you want to become a man?"

He nodded.

"What sort of man do you think you will be?"

"A… A good one?"

"And what is it that makes a man truly good?"

"Kindness?"

She rolled her eyes and scowled at the smudge of blue that was a lake far off in the distance. A Spirit lived there as well, a nasty one who liked to drown naughty little boys. Was his mother deciding whether she should take him to that spirit instead? A shiver drilled straight down to Eoin's bones. He hadn't meant to be naughty, really he hadn't. Now anxious as his pony, he tried to keep from fidgeting so as not to annoy Bronagh further. He stared at her, desperate for her to provide a better clue as to what she wanted to hear. At last, she turned back to him.

"A good man is one who knows his place. Look at the tree, my son. 'Tis a whole made of parts. Each has a purpose, a job to perform. The branches act as branches. The roots act as roots. The leaves and the sap, the fruit and the bark… *They* don't wish to be anything more than what they are! They accept their place and, by working together, help the tree flourish and grow. This is the way of the world. Do you understand?"

He tried to. His whole wee face scrunched up with his efforts, yet he just couldn't seem to connect what she said to what he felt.

"That's fine for the tree, Mother, but men aren't trees."

"We are each born into duty," she sneered, lips tight and thin.

"But—"

"We must faithfully serve the duties that were given to us by the gods, and *your* duty is to the knighthood, as was your father's and his father's before him. 'Tis weakness to deny this. More than that, 'tis wicked."

"But why?"

She smacked the back of his head then stooped to tear a strip of grass-stained fabric from the hem of her skirts. While tying this to the hawthorn, she prayed for the Spirit to cure Eoin of his cowardice. Her voice lowered to a hoarse, mawkish groan as she recounted the agonies she suffered during Eoin's birth and then it crescendoed into a wail as she professed to be afraid that she'd failed in her own duty, which was, of course, to bear worthy sons.

"The shame is more than I can stand! If sinful disobedience be his fate, I beg you, Noble Spirit, kill me now! Strike me dead!"

"No, Mother, please no!" Eoin cried, weeping at her feet.

He left his home and his childhood behind that day. Although he still didn't understand why the world was arranged as it was, he swore to follow the path chosen for him by the gods and let the lesson of the hawthorn shape him into what he was born to be: a weapon. During those transformative years when tempers boil with rebellion, Eoin had simply to remember the smell of wet, crushed grass to cool his blood. If he was ordered to fight, he fought. If he was ordered to kill, he killed, trusting that it was for everyone's benefit. Any doubts remaining were bottled up and thrown away. A weapon does not question the arm that wields it.

Everything was working fine, but then Eoin destroyed it all on a mad whim.

Why? Why had he listened to emotion and not reason? That day in court, he should have agreed with his father or at least one of the other men, yet he'd arrogantly assumed to know better than those a thousand times wiser than he. And just look at the damage that one lapse in judgment had caused! He was disgraced. Crippled. Stranded in a savage land with no chance of escape.

Yet even worse than this was what he'd done to Muireann. To whom could she turn to for support now that he had essentially abandoned her? That wasn't an act of love but selfishness. Had he truly loved her, he would have placed her wishes, her needs, above his own, and what she'd needed from

Eoin most was his continued friendship.

His mother was right. It *was* wicked to reject one's duty. Perhaps that is why it felt so good, why the urge to go against what was expected of him had been so irresistible, for what power did evil have that was more persuasive than temptation?

But... It had felt more than good. It had passed through him like divine inspiration. He'd been so sure that the gods wanted him to have a new purpose, serve a new duty, and if that were the case, then he hadn't been wicked or selfish at all. But... If *that* were the case, why were the gods punishing him so? Eoin huffed. Contradictions and complications. Puzzles that couldn't be solved. He flexed his hands, glaring at them as though they held the answers he sought.

"Are they hurting again?" Cinnia asked.

"No."

"Then whatever's the matter?"

"Nothing. I'm just thinking."

"Thinking? Dear me! I wasn't aware cheese came from thinking."

Eoin looked at her askance. "What?"

"That frown you wear could curdle milk."

She grinned at him expectantly, but Eoin was in no mood to laugh, especially not with the only person he'd ever met who seemed more and more a stranger the more he got to know her. She was the biggest contradiction of all. What was a witch's gods-given purpose? What did she do while she was alone in the woods? Five days had come and gone since he caught her with the creatures that almost ate him, and in that time, his quest for the truth had become an obsession.

"Cinnia," he said, and her breath snagged as it always did whenever he called her by name. "Do you believe we are all born into duty?"

"Is that what's put you out of sorts today? I should have guessed."

Sitting down next to him, she took Eoin's hand and, using the barest brush of a finger, drew circles and swirls across the back of it.

"When your fever was at its height, you talked quite a bit about duty."

"I did?" he asked, forcing himself to concentrate on anything other than the darts of unwanted pleasure that shot through his skin. Tension trapped within his head began to shift, and he clamped his eyes shut just in case it decided to drain from them in tears.

"Mm-hmm. You kept saying that you'd failed, that you deserved to die. I was so sad to hear you speak that way. How could someone like you, someone so…"

She stood up. Eoin watched as she walked a few paces away. Deep in thought, she chewed first on her lip then the tip of her thumbnail.

"Someone so…?" he prompted.

She circled back to him, gaze studious and penetrating.

"Speak your piece, Cinnia. You've more than earned that right."

"Well, 'tis only that you're so sweet. I mean good!" she exclaimed, spotting his scowl. "Um, v-virtuous? That's it. Virtuous. Decent. Especially compared to… And, well, I feel you…you ought to be…gentler with yourself."

"Gentler?"

"Yes."

"*Gentler?*"

Now he laughed, although she didn't seem happy about it. Perhaps it wasn't as 'sweet' as she liked. He supposed she hoped compliments would make him forget that she hadn't even attempted to give him a proper answer. Distract and deflect. She'd made them into an art.

On that fateful night, once she realised what he had seen and they were both pulled in a vertigo rush back to opposite sides of the chasm they'd foolishly tried to bridge, she hadn't explained herself. She had instead stooped to rebuild the fire. What a sneaky, underhanded trick! Not only was it a distraction but also a test. She deliberately moved into a vulnerable position to determine whether Eoin would attack her.

He had certainly wanted to. His enemies were her allies! He'd trusted her, yet she had been deceiving him all along, and he was overcome with the desire to push her down, beat her bloody, make her hurt just as much as he was hurting. Cries for revenge had swirled through Eoin's head like greasy pink foam in a river poisoned by a war upstream, but even so, he'd known full well that he couldn't ever hurt her. It just wasn't in him. He must have failed a few other tests throughout the years, for he was a boy yet, green and gullible and woolgathering, and Cinnia... No. The *witch* had defeated him without so much as lifting a finger.

Devastated, Eoin had then slumped back down onto the bed. Time passed. He wasn't sure how much, but she had eventually crept to his side and placed her hand on his chest, resting it above his heart. At first, he had thought that, for whatever nefarious reason, she was laying claim to him. *He belongs to me*, she'd said to the creatures. However, it was not ownership he sensed in her touch. Her hand shook too much for that, and the weight of its pitiful, pleading desperation had practically bruised him. *Are we still friends*, it had asked. *Will you still tell me stories? After all, you still need me, don't you?*

Aye, he did. Needed her for food, medicine and, yes, protection too, though it stung to admit. Added to this shame was the maddening fact that he was far too susceptible to her charms. Her smile, the sound of her voice, even her smell had wormed their way inside of him and tunnelled through to places which hadn't seen light for many, many years. Long-buried seeds were starting to sprout. Ideas, ridiculous ideas, were beginning to hatch. She was changing him somehow, and the worst part was how easy it would be to surrender to her. But after what Eoin had learned about her on that night, he swore never to let temptation turn his head again.

So they'd spent the last five days locked in a battle of wits. Since Eoin was nowhere near as adept at manipulation as a witch, he was at a disadvantage, yet her desperate touch had shown him that he was not without charms of his own.

"Cinnia?" he now asked her.

Again the catch of breath. "Yes?"

"I have a favour to ask."

Just as predicted, she brightened. When Eoin was a squire, one of his first duties had been to care for the King's hounds. They were massive, shaggy brutes, bred to hunt wolf and man alike, yet despite their intimidating appearance, they were affectionate, loyal, and only too happy to obey when given a command. Eoin was reminded of them as he looked upon Cinnia's beaming face.

"I've noticed how little you've eaten of late. Prithee, do not refute what I can plainly see," he said to counter her wordless protest. "I shall leave you a beggar should this go on."

"You mustn't trouble yourself with such worries. You are weak yet."

He swallowed down the growl climbing his throat. *Not so weak as you think.* "That I am alive at all is thanks to you, and 'tis my wont to repay my debts."

"To see you recover is payment enough."

"Be reasonable. You cannot survive without food."

"Survive?" She half sighed, half scoffed. "Survival has

never been my concern."

That secret pain of hers welled up in her eyes, and Eoin's heart clenched with a pang of conscience. This was treacherous territory. Damn her for figuring out exactly how to exploit his sympathy! He must do something to regain the upper hand.

"Cinnia," he said, rolling her name across his tongue as though savouring its taste. "Cinnia, Cinnia, Cinnia. What am I to do with you?" He chuckled and shook his head, and when he looked at her again, her eyes had dried because she was too enthralled to remember her pain or even how to blink. "I just want to show you how grateful I am for all you've done for me. That's fair, isn't it?"

She quickly agreed. He watched her a while longer in silence. Only when she practically vibrated with the need to please him did he continue.

"I've come up with the perfect solution to our problem. Hoireabard, my horse—"

"Poor darling," she interrupted with a tsk. "He was lovely."

"Aye. Lovely," said Eoin cautiously. This was their first direct acknowledgement of the attack. He had a thousand questions about it that wanted answers but would undoubtedly have better luck asking the creatures themselves. Best to skirt round the issue, keep her compliant. "If you were to go where he fell and retrieve my saddlebags, you will find coin enough to feed us both for a season or more."

"I'm awfully sorry, Eoin, but by now any wealth you had

will be gone. Your belongings will have been picked through just as thoroughly as Hoireabard's bones."

"Really? How strange. I didn't think any of the villagers dared to come this far into the woods."

As soon as he finished saying this, it sprung to mind that the scavengers she alluded to were not of the human variety. One glance at her confirmed his hypothesis. Embarrassment— or was it guilt?—made her droop from head to toe. She'd divulged more than she intended. Her constant longing for his approval would be her undoing, but Eoin's would be his face if he weren't careful. He couldn't let her read anything from it other than confusion. No demands, no accusations; he simply had to ask the helper for help.

"But, Cinnia," he said, dragging a whine along with his words, "what conceivable use have they for such things?"

"Not a one, only they desire all which men desire. Oh, do let's speak of something else! I know. Let me sing for you again. You'll enjoy that, won't you?"

Clever miss. She was right. He *would* enjoy it. Very much so. Her voice was an elixir. Every time she sang, Eoin knew nothing of duty and the danger he was in was a concept far removed from reality. His soul even seemed at times to leap from his body. He imagined it as a rainbowed ray of light that flew away to a golden palace in the sky where he was safe and wanted and home.

To her arms she bids him run.

Forever always to her arms.
Patiently she does await him,
As the moon awaits the sun.
La di dai de lie loo
La di dai de lie lay
How long will she love him?
Forever always.

Eoin shuddered. This wouldn't do. He had to resist. This was part of her magic just as she was part of these evil woods. She was a witch who thrived alongside ghosts and monsters, moving through them as easily as a shepherdess amongst sheep, and now that he required less sleep than before, Eoin was able to track just how often she went out there. She followed no schedule that he could discern, but there was not a single day that went by without her disappearing into that haunted, horrid forest at least once. Unsurprisingly, she never offered to tell Eoin where she had gone or what she'd been doing. It couldn't have been good, though, else she wouldn't have felt the need to keep him in the dark like this.

As if that wasn't ample proof of her depravity, another damning clue came from the behaviour that directly preceded her leaving. She could be eating, talking, or doing any number of other things when suddenly she'd cock her head to the side as though listening to a whisper on the wind, and then she would set her jaw and run off without wasting another second. Something was calling to her soul just as her siren song called to Eoin's, but unlike him, Cinnia didn't even try to fight it.

This should have been more than enough to quash the rebellion in Eoin's mind. But it wasn't. For whenever she returned from the forest, he saw the sorrow in her step. He heard her grief as she wept at night when she believed him asleep. And although he didn't want to, he still felt her pain as sharply as before. Eoin hated that there was such a fine line between friend and foe, and he hated that it was getting harder to tell on which side they currently lay. This latest game they played with each other was a remarkably cruel one. Neither of them could win it, but if Eoin must lose, then he would do so on his own terms.

"Thank you, Cinnia. That was beautiful. You put even the most accomplished of royal bards to shame. Was it your mother who taught you to sing?"

His praise placed a grin onto her lips. The mention of her mother ripped it away again.

"She did a wonderful job," he cheerfully went on just as if Cinnia had replied. "My mother taught me as well, though not as much as my father did, and nothing as sentimental as singing. My education focused on more pragmatic subjects. How to ride, how to hunt and fight. Because a man's highest duty is to provide for those he...cares about."

Her grin returned. It was the most singularly beautiful sight Eoin had ever seen, leaving him dazed until he slapped together enough self-awareness to break free of her spell.

"So you see," he said, after forcing out a cough to disguise his indiscretion. "I can't just lie here and do nothing all day. I need to contribute somehow, do you understand?"

"Of course! I regret not recognising this sooner."

And she really did, didn't she? Regret was written there on her face, plain as day, and it was beyond unfair that it was just as beautiful as her happiness.

"My sword!" he exclaimed and then stifled a groan of exasperation. He hadn't planned to come to the point quite so abruptly, but there was no going back now. "The woods are littered with weapons and…other…wares… Aren't they?"

"Yes," she said, squinting at him in bemusement. Maybe he hadn't made as much a mess of this as he'd feared.

"The creatures mustn't have any desire for those then, do they?"

"…No."

"Then surely they'll have left *my* sword alone, wouldn't they?"

"I suppose."

She frowned. She was starting to get suspicious. Although his sword was what he wanted most, he couldn't let her suss that out, just as he couldn't let her know the actual reason he wanted it so badly.

Steady, Eoin. Choose your next words wisely.

"Then the favour I ask is this: bring me everything of mine that the creatures have left to rot. The sword is of the highest quality and the saddle is made of fine leather, as are the saddlebags. They can be sold in the village for a good amount of food. After I clean and mend them, that is."

"I've told you not to worry about such things."

"And I've told you, I can't rest knowing you go hungry for my sake."

He presented what he hoped was a winning smile. She did not appear convinced, so he stood. Slowly, he walked to where she sat, trying to move as those suave, sought-after swains in court did. It worked. He had her undivided attention, and when he reached out to loop a lock of her silken hair around his fingers, she shivered.

"Will you do this for me, Cinnia? Please?"

A faint nod. Another blissful, breathless grin. Eoin trailed her to the door, watching as she hurried off into the woods, hiding his disgruntled exhaustion until she was out of sight. This had to be the most gruelling battle he'd yet fought. It was almost over now, though. As soon as his sword was back in hand, he wouldn't have time to waste obsessing over siren songs, silly daydreams, or ridiculous ideas.

Cinnia may have wanted to turn back into the girl she had been before the flower was picked, but Eoin was finally going to kill the boy he'd been before the smell of crushed grass once and for all.

CHAPTER 6

here were no sun-dappled afternoons in the Accursed Lands with which to warm one's heart, nor were there crisp breezes to clear troubled minds. It was ever the same dull, lifeless day. The sky was the colour of a storm, stank of mildew, and put too much pressure on the earth. Still, it was good for Eoin to be out of doors. He needed to train, to rebuild muscle and stamina, and he couldn't do that while Cinnia was watching. Her caring nature veered past coddling and headed straight towards smothering whenever Eoin's balance happened to falter. As his patience with her was significantly thinner than it had been before, he'd started waiting until the woods called her away before he moved around much.

But only during the day, never at night. And he only went so far as the edge of Cinnia's yard. This was strategy, not cowardice. Sharpening a dulled weapon took time.

Although she sometimes would remain in the woods for

hours, she wouldn't be gone that long today, so Eoin couldn't work up a good sweat. He jogged around the clearing, careful not to tread over the rows of sickly little sprouts that Cinnia stubbornly refused to let die despite their best efforts. What did the future hold for them and thus for her?

Don't think about it. Stay in the moment. One foot in front of the other. Get on with it.

He walked over to the well, drew water, and drank it as though all his worries were as simple to slake as thirst. His arms felt like they'd been stabbed through with hundreds of needles, but that was just fine with him. It meant he was making progress. A few days ago, it felt like daggers. To further test his strength, he passed the bucket from one hand to the other, lifted it, lowered it, and slowly poured the rest of the water back down into the well, watching as the glittering stream disappeared into the murky depths.

He drew a second bucketful then a third and a fourth, but on the fifth, his arms mutinied. The bucket slipped from his grasp. What a damnable nuisance! He glowered at his hands as if to scare off the tremors. This obviously didn't work, so his focus shifted to the trees. Their branches were like hands themselves, straining to reach him. A fetid gust of wind hissed through withered leaves, and he could almost hear a scheming, poisonous whisper bidding him closer.

"You'll have me soon enough," he grumbled to it.

He meant what he said. Death prowled these woods, as

demanding of blood as a changeling is of swindled milk, and it was going to suck Eoin dry. That is what *his* future held in store for him. There was no denying it. The gods were owed this penance. He wasn't their chosen one. He would not save the kingdom, nor would he win Muireann's love or his family's respect. He'd been careless, too preoccupied with flights of fancy to see that arrogance deceived him. But things were different now. He had made peace with his lot. He accepted that he'd never leave this accursed place. The only hope he allowed for was the hope to deal the reigning evil some measure of damage before he succumbed to its brutal appetite.

"Why, isn't this a surprise! I thought you'd have gone back to sleep," Cinnia gaily chirped to him as she emerged from the tangle.

Her slender arms were laden with the relics of Eoin's former life, and he stared at the gore splattered over them. It had mingled with the creatures' filth and, regardless of the weeks that had passed since the attack, was still sticky. That was fitting. It was ugly evidence of his utter failure after all. Eoin deserved to be confronted with it over and over and over again. He thought it odd, though, that he wasn't repelled by the sight. It did not hurt him in the least to look at it. Did Death already own that much of him that he'd gone dead inside? No. He knew he was very much alive because the sludge had spread itself onto Cinnia's arms and this, he could not abide. It tore at him like a ravenous ghoul. Grunting, Eoin grabbed Cinnia and dragged her to the well. She yelped in fright, but when he began to scrub her clean, her alarm melted into sympathetic understanding.

"No need to fret. A bit of mess doesn't bother me."

Her assurances merely drew his attention to her mouth and then to a lurid smear across her cheek. Biting back another grunt, he used wetted palms to wash off every last trace of blood. Then the task was done, yet Eoin kept hold of her face, his thumbs stroking astonishingly smooth skin. He couldn't help himself. He gazed into her eyes. It struck him anew, how changeable they were, how they reflected all the various men he'd been to her. The adversary. The invalid. The companion. The...

He glanced away because this latest reflection was a grievous distortion. It must be. Had to be. It was too perfect to be real, and similarly perfect illusions had already swept him off his feet too many times. Help was within reach, though. Cinnia had carried it back from the woods, unaware that she brought him the very means to free himself from her wicked influence. His sword. A physical reminder of his duty, his purpose, and his true self. He rushed to take it up from the pile. The weight of it was uncomfortable yet calming. He swung it through the air then altered his voice to take on the same gruff inflexion of his father.

"Thank you. For fetching my belongings. Keep what you like. Use it, trade it, I don't really care."

"Eoin, I—"

"'Tis the least I can offer, but *all* I offer."

Tightening his grip on the sword, he chanced to look at her and, for his sake as much as hers, did not remark upon the quiver in her lips. He *must* think as his father would. It was the only way to break her hold on him.

"I sincerely do apologise for any confusion I may have inadvertently caused. I never intended to mislead you, and I can appreciate how those without, ah, let's say proper breeding, might...misconstrue certain interactions they may have with their betters when the judgment of those, ahem, aforementioned betters is impaired. As mine was. By severe injury. Additionally, I want it noted that I do consider you a...a sort of friend, one might say. In spite of..."

"In spite of what?" Her brow rose. Her beauty hardened. Without warning, she had reverted into the ferocious queen of the wilds that he'd first met, transcendent and terrifying, and she observed Eoin with regal disgust. "You must be very pleased with yourself. What fine sport you've had at my expense."

"Truly, Cinnia, I am sorry. I didn't mean to hurt you."

"So you think you've hurt me, do you? Hah! Nothing you could possibly do would match what I have yet endured."

His fellow men cautioned that the fairer sex, like the fair folk, favoured riddles above all else, but Eoin, having limited experience with women, wasn't prepared for this type of fight.

He didn't have a single clue what to say that Cinnia wouldn't turn against him, so he stayed mum as she railed.

"You think I'm in love with you, is that it? You take me for a simple-minded girl who cannot help but admire you. There must be many such girls where you come from. Girls like your blessed Muireann."

A peal of thunder crashed through Eoin's head. "What? How do you—?"

"Am I wrong? Muireann isn't your sweetheart? Hmm, perhaps not. Not if she let you wander off like a ninny to countless dangers."

"Stop."

"Though maybe she was happy to see the last of you."

"I warn you, hold your tongue."

"Poor, poor, lovelorn little boy. 'Oh, Muireann, my darling, my dove,'" she said, mockingly wringing her hands and batting her eyelashes. "'Oh, Muireann, Muir—'"

"Be quiet!" The wall of trees caught his anger and bounced it around the clearing.

When the echoes faded, Cinnia smirked. "Did you forget that you confided your every dream whilst in fever? You bared your soul to me as I cradled you in my arms. I know you, Eoin, intimately so, but do not presume to know the first thing about me."

"I wouldn't be quite so proud of the secrets I keep if I were you."

FOR THE LOVE OF A WITCH

She gestured in exaggerated pantomime that he continue. Infuriated, he ignored the warning gnawing at his gut.

"I know you are compelled day and night to answer a dark summons out there in the woods. It must be ungodly magic indeed for it to bring even a witch like you to tears."

Cinnia slapped him with the force of a cracking whip. He ran his tongue along the corner of his mouth, tasting the sting, while she gaped at her handiwork with wondering consternation.

Then she feigned laughter and said, "I've been a fool to believe you were, by some miracle, different than... I see now you are just as cruel a man as the rest."

"Aye, you are a fool if you judge honesty as cruelty. Would you think better of me had I continued to pretend you aren't what we both know you are?"

"And what am I?! What is my crime? How have I sinned? Or is my sheer existence so abhorrent that you can't find it within yourself to treat me with even a shred of the kindness I've shown you?"

She spun away. Her hands were fists, her knuckles white. She swayed, choking on stifled sobs. This wasn't what Eoin wanted. It was horrible, vulgar, and if another had been the cause of it, he'd have had their head. His sword was suddenly too heavy to hold. He let it drop to the ground. Now acting entirely on impulse, he threw his arms around her and planted a swift, hard kiss onto her hair.

"No!" she cried as she shoved him off. "Don't taunt me with what I can't have! Can't you tell that you're destroying the only piece of me that's left? Go! I want you gone! Leave me to my misery and go!"

"Are you trying to drive me mad? Why do you say such things?"

"Because that's all you deserve, you clumsy child!"

Her ire withered upon slackened lips, for just then she cocked her head in the manner Eoin had come to loathe. She cast him one final black look and then walked to the trees. With every step she took, a voice inside of him howled until it could not be ignored. He didn't know whether it was curiosity or pride that compelled him, but he leapt after her.

"I will have the truth!" he yelled, seizing her wrist. "Whose call do you answer?"

She pushed and pulled and beat against him, crazed as a fox in a snare. "Let me go! You must let me go!"

"Whose call do you answer?"

"Please!"

"Tell me his name!"

"You already know!" she wailed as though it physically hurt her to admit even this much.

Even if it did, so be it. It hurt him too, so let them bleed together if that's what it took to finally and completely cut through her web of deceit. With his free hand, Eoin grabbed her by the chin, forcing her to look at him, to see the man that was not going to allow a mere spider like her to get the best of him.

"Say it, Cinnia! Say his name!"

She moaned in despair. All at once, the life went out of her, and as glass filled her eyes, she said, "The Beast."

And there it was. The confirmation of his utmost fear. It ripped through him with such savage intensity that he all but fainted. He clung to Cinnia, both to steady himself and to prevent her escape. She started fighting again. She was also cringing, wincing, and Eoin realised that her master must somehow be able to tell that she wasn't on her way to him yet.

"What's he saying?" he growled to her. "What does he want from you?"

"Please, I have to hurry!"

"You're not going anywhere."

"You don't understand! I have to go! He doesn't like to be kept waiting!"

"Then take me to him."

She gave a dull, humourless chuckle. She doubted him, didn't she? Just as many others did. His father. His mother. The peasants. Even Muireann. Especially Muireann. They all perceived some fault in him, some fatal flaw. What did they say behind closed doors? Did they call him a weakling? A disappointment too dim-witted to be a coward? And now here was this witch—*this witch*—marking him as so trivial a threat to her beloved Beast that she raised Eoin from the dead for nought but her own sick amusement.

This would not stand.

He yanked Cinnia back to where his sword lay, picked it up, and repeated his demand. Mesmerised by the blade, she almost laughed again but then became a trembling, tender thing, not unlike a flower struggling to survive an early frost. Her lips drained of colour. She touched her fingers to them and then stretched those same fingers towards Eoin, stopping just short of his cheek. She seemed to live a lifetime in those few moments and found the years bleak and unforgiving.

"He'll kill you," she managed to rasp.

"I don't care."

Her expression darkened. She lunged forward and drove her nails into Eoin's shoulder, into the troublesome wounds that still hadn't fully healed. Searing pain sent him to his knees. He clutched shuddering, screaming flesh and glared at her in wordless outrage as she sputtered apologies.

"I won't let you fight him, Eoin! I can't watch you die!"

"You don't have a choice!"

In the same instant, they turned to his fallen sword. She scooped it up before he could, which made him tumble onto his face. While he breathed dirt, she dashed to the well and flung the sword in. Then she was gone, racing into the woods, her hair flying out behind her like a banner as she rushed to obey the Beast.

Cursing her name, Eoin hauled himself to his feet to run

after her.

CHAPTER 7

The hunt was on. Cinnia was the fleet-footed deer, Eoin the baying hound. Following close behind was a host of murdered men whose uncanny horns blared in Eoin's ears, demanding the vengeance they'd long been craving. Some distant part of his mind knew it was absurd to go where Cinnia unwillingly led, but Eoin was in thrall to the chase. His blood pumped so wildly that he tasted his heart in his mouth. He felt light, lighter than he had in weeks. But this was a lie. His body betrayed him, not with weakness but with an imitation of strength.

Yet he didn't care whether it was death he hunted. Let it come. He would roar into its face. Yes, roar, as he had when he struck fear into the horde even while broken and bleeding. And where exactly were those wicked imps hiding now? Did they watch from the treetops or dank, stinking holes? Were they about to swoop down on him? It mattered not. He was ready. He wanted this as he'd never wanted anything before. He was a young god of the wood, angry and hungry, and only the ritual, only the blood, could appease him.

As he ran, he crushed any bone lying in his way into dust. He passed the last of Hoireabard's sorry remains but didn't see them. His eyes were locked on the shock of red that was Cinnia's hair. She called for him to stop, to go back, and then she saved what was left of her breath to try to outpace him, but this was pointless. He gained on her with each step.

The trees thinned until nothing was left of them save a carpet of charcoal. The skeletons here were intact and spread out as they'd fallen. They were gnarled, screaming atrocities, roasted by what must have been a raging inferno, and they were everywhere, draped over slabs of stone or monstrously conjoined in lumps of petrified fat. Charred weaponry quilled the battlefield. Eoin slowed to grab at a mace, only to have its handle crumble into ash.

Cinnia navigated through the corpses flawlessly and increased her lead, but Eoin spied her destination. There, at the centre of the carnage, the earth was cleaved in two. It was like the leering mouth of a titan. Tendrils of smoke slipped out from between teeth made of jutting, splintered rock and fouled the sky. He had reached the lair of the Beast.

Whirling around, Cinnia held out her hands, again bidding him stop. "Please, don't! Don't come any closer! Wait there, Eoin, please, I'm begging you! I promise to explain everything if only you'll just wait for me there!"

But she must have seen it in his eyes—the murderous, feverish gleam—and decided nothing would change his mind. She said something else that he didn't hear and then clambered down into the mouth of rock and disappeared from sight.

The ghosts whipping at his heels retreated, slinking back into the ether, but before they did, they insisted Eoin look to his feet. There lay a sword just in front of them, whole and unburnt. It evidently had belonged to a great hero, for it was decorated with emeralds and the ivory of sea creatures. He bent to retrieve it, peeling away the brittle black fingers which still clung to its hilt. The sword fit his hand so perfectly he allowed himself a smile. This was a gift. A sign from the gods.

Exhilarated, he too plunged into the titan's mouth. It was a cavern that descended into darkness. Filth trickled from its walls of rubble, splashing onto more wealth than Eoin had imagined even in the most extravagant of his fantasies. Coin and jewels, strings of pearls, bars of gold; a kingdom's fortune squandered beneath layers of soot and slop. Eoin's face twitched in anger. So many years of horror inflicted upon so many people, all for the sake of greed. If he had doubts, if even a piece of him yearned to escape this obscene place while he had the chance, his righteous rage drowned them all out.

Light shone in the distance. Glittering red against the Beast's hoard, it burned ever brighter as Eoin travelled further down into the earth. It was hotter here, the heat wetter. It pressed into Eoin's throat along with the snaking smoke, choking him, but between coughs, he heard a familiar voice.

Cinnia.

She was pleading to someone. She whimpered on and on, sounding like the trill of a cursed flute or a dying songbird. Eoin almost let her distract him long enough that reason unmoored his bravery, but this was a test. He refused to let anything stand in his way. Especially her, the traitor. The witch.

He sprinted forward. The cavern expanded, distended into a vast, subterranean cathedral. Rancid water oozed from the ceiling and puddled on the floor, and hellfire blazed all around, rising up from bottomless pits. There was treasure here too, oceans of it, swelled into mounds thrice Eoin's height.

And there she was. On her knees, hands clasped in supplication. "Please, my Lord, let him live. I beseech you, Mightiest of Kings, show him mercy. Let him live, and he will spend his days praising you."

"Never!" cried Eoin, holding his new sword aloft. "Face me, thou most wretched of demons, and I shall cleanse the world of your vile poison. Face me, for your day of reckoning is at hand!"

There was no answer save for the drip of water and the roar of the flames. Then a great, rumbling tremor shook the ground. Eoin struggled to stay upright. Cinnia toppled over onto the precious hoard, and there she remained, though her prayer continued.

"Please, oh please, my Lord, my powerful Lord, please let

him live, please…"

The rumbling rolled on. It wasn't the shifting of rocks, as Eoin first thought, but deep, low, monstrous laughter. Suddenly, the burning pits exploded. Eoin had to shield himself from the treasure pelting his head and from the flash of fire that threatened to blind him. When next he looked up, he could do nothing but stare at the mountainous creature climbing out of the abyss.

Rusted brown scales as hard as rock. Claws as long as spears. Teeth thick as trees and sharper than any blade known to man. Two massive crimson eyes stared at Eoin with malicious glee, and it was as though the entrance to the lair, that strange titan-like formation, had been nothing more than a pale imitation of the smoking, frothing mouth of the dragon that was now grinning down at Eoin.

Terror strangled him. His sword danced in the air. His body buckled as if it meant to run even without him commanding it to do so. But he wasn't going to run. The smell of crushed grass wouldn't let him.

So Eoin roared.

After a moment's surprise, the Beast threw back his gargantuan head, and the world trembled with his laughter. "Well met, little knight! Well met, indeed."

It was hopeless from the start.

The Beast smiled as Eoin rushed forward, and just the

slightest flick of his spiked tail sent Eoin soaring. He smashed into rock with a thud. More of that seismic laughter buried him beneath an avalanche of treasure. The Beast then waited, watching with detached interest while Eoin struggled up from the golden pile. Fire licked at his yellow, nightmarish fangs, and although he could have effortlessly incinerated Eoin, he did not. This wasn't a battle. It was a game.

Eoin spat out a mouthful of blood and charged once more. Again, he was thrown back. And then again. With each assault, he became slower to rise. All of his many years of training were for nought. He was helpless, utterly helpless. Though he continued to charge, primal fear coursed through his quivering limbs. He had no words, no thoughts. They'd been stolen from him as though made of the same sparkling wealth the Beast so coveted. Without them, Eoin was no longer a man. He was an animal, wounded and shrieking, and his sword served as bared teeth, snarling, snapping, frantic to catch flesh.

But there was none to be found. The Beast's plated hide was impenetrable. Then, having already grown bored with his new plaything, the Beast lunged, quick as lightning despite his enormous size. He pinned Eoin under his paw and, as if studying its effects, began to apply incremental amounts of pressure. Whilst gravity poured into his head, Eoin gawked at the calamity lording over him. The veins in his eyes burst in a succession of soft pops, and he couldn't blink the blood away fast enough to see anything but red. Pain and panic writhed together within his chest like a rat king biting at itself. Madness was conjured from the mix. As the Beast lowered his serpentine neck, Eoin listened to the screams of a dying man, too far gone to realise that they came from him.

"Ah, how sweet," the Beast purred, sucking in Eoin's scent through flaring nostrils.

Then surprisingly, the pressure disappeared. He could move again. Rolling to his side, Eoin gulped for air until slowly, very slowly, both breath and brain returned to him. He lifted his head and through the blood seeping from his eyes, he saw Cinnia. She stood with her back to him, arms outstretched, face upturned, her hair blown about by the heat of the inferno. She was chanting like a priestess caught in the midst of ancient, unspeakable worship, and every second of it was another knife stabbed into Eoin's heart.

"My beautiful Lord, my one true God, how I love you, how I ache for you…"

The Beast let out a blistering sigh. "Tread lightly, whore, lest you annoy me."

"My beautiful Lord," she crooned again, curving her arms in an invitation to embrace. He spat a fine rain of embers down upon her head in reply. Once the last spark had hissed against her skin, she said, "I merely wish to serve you as I have always done. I think only of your glory."

"Pretty words, though they do nothing to stave off my hunger."

"Oh, but *he* isn't a worthy meal, my Lord! Don't grant him such an honourable end. He doesn't deserve it. Why not force him to live, most splendid King, that he may carry the shame of his defeat forever? The world grows complacent. Make him remind them of your majesty."

The Beast's stony brow furrowed as he contemplated this, but then he seized Cinnia, hoisting her up to meet the level of his burning eyes. She was a witch. A traitor to all of mankind. She'd done this to herself, yet Eoin couldn't stop from crying out.

"How quaint," the Beast chortled. "It calls for you. It squeaks your name."

Twisting in his clawed clutches, she looked at Eoin for the first time since he entered the lair. All colour had left her. She was disturbingly white, but it was what he saw in her face that cost him his breath again. He saw the truth in it. She *wasn't* a witch at all. Though servant to an evil master, Cinnia was herself innocent of any wrongdoing. She was, always had been, doing whatever it took to protect Eoin. Awash with relief and with gratitude, he wanted nothing else now but to hold his gentle friend, tell her that he was sorry for doubting her, and then die with her.

"Look how it reaches for you! What a funny little morsel."

"My Lord, I—"

The Beast threw Cinnia down. Eoin didn't have enough left in him to even crawl to her side, although he was determined to try. He dragged himself forward. When he again cried her name, it seemed she wanted to run to him, but the Beast stood between them. And he wasn't done with her.

"For many days, you've come to me with its scent on your skin, and now you beg for its life? Faithless slut. Have I been negligent in your instruction? Is it you, and not the world, who has grown complacent?"

"No, my handsome and wise King, I remember well every lesson you've ever taught me."

"That can't be true, else you wouldn't dare take a lover," he said, grumbling as a spoiled, sulking child.

"Dearest Lord, you misunderstand. I care for him, yes, but 'tis a...*mother's* heart with which I beg. He's just a boy! I pity him as any woman would a mewling babe."

"Lies!"

"I swear it! My heart belongs to you alone! I am yours! Completely and eternally yours!"

The Beast's mighty roar blasted through the cavern, knocking stalactites loose from overhead. They plummeted into the lake of fire, and magma splashed all about, yet the Beast didn't care that it liquefied the treasure it touched. He only had concern for but one of his possessions. Gnashing his teeth, he again spat embers at Cinnia. The length of his neck was incandescent with rage, glowing red then orange then yellow, brighter and brighter still, until it was agony to behold. Suddenly, he turned his head towards Eoin, and a ferocious spurt of fire flew from his mouth. Eoin's body at last cooperated, fear supplying him with the speed required to dive to safety. The Beast stormed after him through the curtain of flames. Another jet of fire came close to devouring Eoin, but that was not the intent. He was shepherded into a corner. The flames were too high and too violent to jump over. There was no escape. He was trapped.

"Watch carefully, whore!" the Beast thundered. "Watch your lover die, and thank me for it!"

"Stop, please! I'll do anything! I will give you anything!"

"Imbecile! I already own everything you have."

Eoin was lost in the hatred of the evil, reptilian eyes glaring down at him. The Beast's behemoth chest expanded and deflated while he stoked the fire within. Bracing himself, Eoin awaited the inevitable.

Cinnia's voice rang out like a bell. "I have one thing left to me yet, my Lord! For his life, I shall give you another!"

"No," Eoin whispered. Then, wailing, he tried to breach the flames which kept him captive. "Don't hurt her! Take me, kill me!"

But it was too late. The Beast spun back to her, and despite the searing heat, Eoin's blood ran cold, because as the Beast moved, he shrunk in size. His body contorted. His armoured hide appeared in some places to implode while in others it burst. And soon, where there had been a dragon, there stood a man. He was tall and well-muscled, solid as a warrior, imposing as a king, but a monster through and through. His skin wasn't skin at all. It was made of the same rusted scales that covered his other form. His nose was too flat to be human, his eyes too large and mouth too wide.

"Are you certain the boy is worth it?" he laughed to Cinnia. "You know how this takes its toll on you."

She kissed him in answer. Vomit bathed Eoin's tongue and painted his feet. The Beast grabbed a handful of her hair, viciously yanking her aside, and sniffed as though he could not only smell Eoin's sick but found it appetising.

He threw Eoin a skeletal grin. "You are blessed, little knight, for you shall bear witness to a true miracle." To Cinnia, he said, "Is it with your own free will that you make this most sacred of pacts?"

"Yes!"

"Then drink, my beauty! Drink!"

In one fluid motion, he slashed his wrist open with his teeth. Cinnia pulled the wound to her lips. As she swallowed mouthful after mouthful of his oozing black blood, the Beast sighed and moaned, all the while staring into Eoin's horrified eyes.

But the horror was only beginning.

CHAPTER 8

y the time the Beast retired to the abyss, Eoin had screamed himself mute. It was with a mangled, exhausted heart that he watched Cinnia collect her clothing. She too was without words yet gifted him with smiles, though they were wavering, spiritless things. Eoin hated himself more with each one.

She approached his cage, and they stared at one another through the bars of fire. She opened her mouth to speak. Eoin cast down his eyes. He'd never been so ashamed or felt less of a man. He sank to his knees. She said his name, and it broke him.

A while later, when he was finally able to raise his head, he found his prison less secure than before. Cinnia held out her hand. He still couldn't look at her. Instead, he passed his gaze over the silver and the gold and the rest of the glittering riches. Lying amongst them was the sword plucked from the wreckage outside. Such a perfect weapon. His sign from the gods. Hah!

That was just a lie he'd told himself. One of many.

"Come to me, Eoin."

Numbed and yet aching, he passed through the dwindling flames. Although Cinnia immediately enfolded him within her arms, guilt weighed his down so that he couldn't return the gesture. Drawing back, she smoothed sweat-soaked hair from his temples and searched his face. He couldn't think what she hoped to find there. Surely everything he used to be was gone.

"Let's go. Some fresh air will do you good."

Maybe she was right, but the burning lake in which the Beast slumbered seemed more inviting than the world above. He stepped to its edge.

"Don't, Eoin, please."

The tremor in her voice distracted him from the fire. He looked her in the eyes and saw her— truly saw her—for what was perhaps the first time. She was a scared little girl hanging on to a thread's worth of composure, a soul so battered there was almost nothing left of it. Eoin had never been a man of words. Hoping she would hear what he was too inept to say, he kissed her cheek and breathed her name against her flushed skin as though it was a prayer. Her body quivered like a sparrow's breast as she cleaved to him. If he could, he would have held her like this forever, but before long, she untangled herself from his embrace. After fussing with his hair again, she led him outside.

It was a moist, windless night. The ghosts brooded in

frosted moonlight that shone down onto their corpses, and he felt their wrath curl around his feet, ordering him to stay and join their eternal watch. His pace slowed. Cinnia squeezed his hand.

"Would you care for a song? One last song before…"

"Before what?"

"Our goodbyes."

He froze. She continued ahead, her smile a wounded animal struggling for escape.

"Wait! Cinnia, you can't just expect me to leave. Not after—"

"You're alive. The rest doesn't matter."

"Of course it does! He raped you! Because of me, your innocence was stolen!"

"Innocence?" She scoffed. "With how often he calls for me, you can't honestly believe I had any innocence left."

He reeled as if dealt a mortal blow, and she tsked with pity.

"You really didn't know, did you? Oh, my sweet boy. Were you, in your happy kingdom so far away, never told of what stopped him all those years ago? Why do you think he agrees to stay underground when he can easily conquer the entire earth? Me, Eoin," she said, thumping a half-closed hand against her chest. "'Tis because of me. I am both his slave and wife. I do what I must to please him, to help him sleep, as I've done since I was forced to wed him."

Was it true? Could she be the reason that Eoin and his

countrymen had not met with the same fate as those in the Accursed Lands? And while he had lain safely within her bed, imagining the worst of her, had she actually been…? Damn him! How could he not have seen it sooner? Perhaps he couldn't have guessed that she was submitting herself to a brutal and relentless illusion of passion, but he should have realised that something was terribly wrong. He should have been able to read it in Cinnia's face, in her eyes. That scared little girl he just discovered hadn't been that hard to find. She'd always been there, pleading for Eoin to trust her, to understand her, yet he had stubbornly chosen otherwise.

Blurting out one apology after another, he tugged her close, but she didn't surrender to him as in that briefest of moments in the lair. She stiffened, and when it became apparent he wasn't going to let her go, she pulled free.

As he followed her to her cottage, Eoin pictured all of the times she'd made this walk alone. At the end of his darkest days, he could always count on finding someone willing to talk of things significant or trivial or with whom to sit in sociable silence. There was comfort in company. But no one ever sat with Cinnia, did they? No one offered to share even this little of her burden. It wasn't fair. He reached for her again. Brushing him aside, she retrieved two gold coins from the folds of her dress. He frowned when she thrust them into his hand.

"Take them," she said. "Use them to travel home to your

Muireann."

The coins bounced off his boot as he dropped them to the ground. Clucking her tongue, she bent to pick them from the weeds, but then she gasped. Her knees buckled. Eoin hurried to steady her before she collapsed.

"I'm fine," she insisted, swatting him away.

"Come inside. You should rest."

"I said I'm fine! You—" Another gasp. She reshaped it through gritted teeth into a growl and turned from Eoin, saying, "Farewell and safe journey."

She had gone but three steps before he scooped her up into his arms.

"Put me down!"

"Hush."

Carrying her inside, he laid her upon the bed. She struggled to rise, and he gently pushed her back, whispering that she needn't be afraid, that he meant her no harm. This only made her roll towards the wall and begin to cry, so with one hand in her hair and another on her shoulder, he closed his eyes, again wishing for her to feel what was trapped inside him, though it was no use.

"Tell me what's wrong. What should I do? How can I help?"

"You can't," came the grim reply. "Eoin, your life is mine twice over. I've learned little of the ways of noble men, but I do know this means you are indebted to me, yes?"

He agreed reluctantly, leery of what she'd say next.

"Then repay that debt and *leave!*"

"No."

"Coward!" She twisted round to glare daggers at him. Spittle flew from her mouth as she yelled, "Hypocrite! You speak endlessly of duty, yet you now refuse to honour it?"

"Don't you dare try to use that against me! I never asked to be saved!"

"Well, neither did I!"

A convulsion of pain crashed through her body as though she'd taken a fit. His breath caught with hers while they waited for it to pass, and this starved their fiery anger down to ashes.

"Cinnia, please! What's happening to you?" he begged, pressing kisses into her hand as she had pressed coins into his.

"Just go away," she groaned.

"Forgive me, but that's the one thing I can never do."

"If you think this mercy, you are sorely mistaken."

It may not have been mercy, and judging by her distress, it may not have even been kind, but to leave her now was unconscionable. Thus, Eoin knelt at her side, cooing the sort of sweet nothings generally reserved for those near death. He lit the fire. Fetched her water. He combed through her knotted hair and washed the sweat from her neck.

Night faded into a colourless dawn. Cinnia wept until exhaustion dried her tears and the latest, most terrible of her secrets was exposed. Had Eoin not been so very weary himself, it might have come as more of a shock. It could have even driven him mad, he supposed, but he hadn't the energy to spare for such theatrics. He accepted the situation without question because at least it explained why he'd been so upset when he stared into the eyes of the attacking horde. Each of those hateful creatures was, like the Beast, made of fang and scale and horn, yet those eyes…

Those eyes were human. They were the one thing inherited, not from their abhorrent excuse of a father, but from their mother.

Cinnia grasped the repugnant swell of her belly as another contraction ravaged her. The life for whom Eoin's was spared was eager to arrive.

Her screams were a torture he couldn't withstand for much longer. Heavy doors and the swishing skirts of the women who hurried in and out of them had always muted the ruthless reality of birth. The most Eoin had ever contributed was to stay out from underfoot as soon as the commotion started. He cursed himself that he hadn't learned more about it, but those were ordinary babies born to ordinary mothers. Assisting in even a thousand such births would not have prepared him for this.

There was so much blood. Too much. It streamed down her legs in trickles and then in rivers while she feverishly prowled the room. She was so pale that she shimmered like snow and he could trace the blue streak of every vein beneath her skin. But it was the noise—the gruesome, wet ripping he heard between screams—that worried him more than anything else. It was as though she were being devoured from within, that the dragon spawn feasted on her innards just as its brothers had done to his horse, as they'd nearly done to Eoin.

Her belly suddenly lurched. Her cries rose to an even more harrowing pitch. She clawed at herself, and he rushed to strip her of the sodden rags she wore then eased her onto her knees. The bloated moon of flesh hung between them, churning and rolling like a tumultuous sea, and the blood gushing from between her shuddering legs became a drowning tide.

"Go," she bawled, though her arms were braced against his, and, despite everything, Eoin couldn't help but laugh because something like a bubble burst within him and the pressure needed releasing somehow. Then he was looking into her delirious, desperate eyes while she stared pleadingly back into his.

"Push," he instructed, and she obeyed. And again and again, until he saw the demon's purple crown emerge. "Push, Cinnia."

She bore down with all she had left. He caught the slippery mass as it slid free. At first, he thought it dead, for it gave no cry, and as he was afraid to face the horrible likeness of its father, he didn't want to check if it breathed. Yet when he braved a peek, he discovered it was human. Completely human. He clapped it on its back. Mottled, ashy skin turned pink as the babe began to wail.

"Oh, Cinnia," he whispered in awe. "Cinnia, look! A son!"

She had no strength with which to respond. Having collapsed against Eoin, she panted for air until it snared in her throat, and with one final push, she expelled a caul of black blood from her womb in a spattering lump. The putrid mess hissed and sizzled as it disappeared into the dirt.

"…shouldn't be here," she mumbled. "Shouldn't see…"

Her eyelids fluttered as moth wings. Her head dipped and bobbed. Sleep barrelled down on her whether she wanted it or not. With the child tucked in his arm, he helped Cinnia inch into the bed and heaped blankets over her. Her face was drawn, her cheeks hollowed. Where heat had poured from her skin, there was now a glacial chill. Even the redness of her hair had dulled. With each passing second, she seemed that much closer to death, but when Eoin tested her pulse, he felt it beating steady as a war drum.

She coughed out what could have been either a laugh or a moan. "…s'all right. Won't die. Not yet. Give…"

He laid the boy upon her. "He's beautiful. Just like his mother."

But was he? And if so, then why?

These questions could wait. The abomination that had fathered the child didn't matter, nor did the violence of its conception or birth. Cinnia kissed the soft pink head over and again, and even after she succumbed to a swoon, still kept her lips pressed against it. *She loves it*, Eoin marvelled, and because she could, his own heart stirred. He stroked a path from the baby's cheek down to its hand where the tiny fingers curled around his.

"Don't," Cinnia whispered, roused by his chuckles. "He isn't yours to love."

"I didn't mean any—"

She tried to rise. "…build a fire."

"Rest now. I'll tend to everything."

Putting up no further argument, she dove into a fitful slumber. Eoin stepped outside into the grey light, stretching his aching back. Though he tried not to dwell on it, it hurt that she sought to push him away after all they'd suffered together. But he deserved it, didn't he? For what he had done to her and what she'd done to protect him. He came here to rid the realm of the evil infesting it, yet thanks to his carelessness, that evil had further spread.

"Gods forgive me."

The gods didn't answer, but something else did. It snarled at Eoin. His body recognised the sound before his mind, and gooseflesh broke out across the nape of his neck. Hidden by the trees, Cinnia's children encircled the cottage. Perhaps they'd been listening to the birth of their brother, or maybe they were simply drawn to the smell of blood. Either way, Eoin was no longer troubled by their presence. They weren't here to harm Cinnia, and if they wanted his life, he wouldn't fight them for it. He calmly gathered kindling for the fire, providing them plenty of chances to attack. They remained as watchers only. He attempted to number them but, remembering the speed with which they moved, gave this up. There were at least three, he knew. He had blinded one, torn the wings of another, and then there was the biggest of them all, the one which was an eerily exact miniature of the Beast.

Except for the eyes. Underneath all that madness, they were her eyes still.

His arms full, he ducked under the deerskin flap and found Cinnia suckling the babe at her breast. They didn't speak while he revived the cinders into flames, but soon Cinnia started to hum. As ever, her voice was the cure his soul craved. All the worry that kept him on his feet melted away, and it was almost impossible to remain awake even a moment more. Crawling next to the bed, he reached up his hand. A little frisson of relief went through him when she clasped it within her own.

"You will recover?"

"Yes," she answered on the edge of a sigh.

"And the boy?"

"In a day's time or less, the Beast will call for him. It would be best you were gone by then."

He lifted himself so that he could look her in the face. "Cinnia, I am unworthy of your pity, but I beg for it once more. A man who would turn his back on you is no man at all.

If you send me from you now, I am lost."

"Better that than death, for death is all that awaits you here. Either the Beast will kill you, or you will kill yourself. I've seen it happen... I've seen... My mother, she..."

She dissolved into tears. The babe, sensing her distress, took up the cry as well. Eoin wrapped his arms around them, kissing them and whispering assurances until they quieted, but while the child was soothed, Cinnia was not.

"Your sympathy is wasted on us," she said into his hair. "We belong to the Beast. I will serve him for the rest of my days, and this poor darling will be fed to the flames. From them, he'll rise in the image of his father, just as each of my other children has."

"No," Eoin mouthed in dismay and held her closer.

"That is why you must go. Not as punishment, never that, but to save you from all the ways my master can hurt you. And there are so many ways."

"There's nothing which can stop him?" he asked her stubbornly, stupidly.

"I've told you already: *I* stop him. Or at the least, I slow him. He has designs on this world, and I keep him entertained enough that he doesn't rush to complete them."

"But why must this burden fall to you?"

She dragged her knuckles lightly across the span of his collarbone. "You asked me if we are born into duty, do you remember? I believe that we are. I was born to be his. And you, Eoin, you were born to show me what I protect. Every time I feel as though it would be better to die, I'll think of you. Your memory will lend me the courage to carry on."

"No, this cannot happen. I won't allow it!" he exclaimed, pulling back to clutch her upper arms, then sobbed from how fragile, how birdlike, they seemed in his hands. "Come away with me! I'll take you both where he won't find you."

"You still don't understand. I imagine that's because you come from a place where good can prevail against all odds, but good doesn't even exist here. I've tried to run. Others have tried to hide me. Always it ends with death." Her wistful gaze dropped to her son. "Or with life."

Sleep was welcomed company that day yet fickle, flitting away as swiftly as it arrived. Eoin barely began to dream before piercing cries jolted him awake again. Just as the father was an unrelenting tyrant, so too was the son.

Though purple bruises bloomed beneath Cinnia's eyes, she was a doting mother. She couldn't keep from kissing her baby and breathing his tender, petal-soft skin as if to memorise its scent. Eoin soon came to realise that she was trying to bestow a lifetime of love before the Beast collected what was his. But did this sweet boy actually belong to him?

"He looks like any other child."

Cinnia hummed an agreement.

"How is this possible?"

"'Tis old magic. Blasphemous magic. The Beast shouldn't be able to create, only destroy, but the blood he makes me drink enthrals my body so that his seed takes root. Now the child is born, the Beast will curse him with hellfire to strip him of his humanity, and, well, you've seen the others." Somehow hearing the question Eoin dared not ask, she added, "This is our seventh son." And when pity stayed his tongue once more, she again answered what he left unspoken. "He would have dozens were he able. Hundreds. He'd command armies could he alone work the spell. Fortunately, more than his desire is needed."

"You must consent," Eoin said, having puzzled this detail out on his own.

"Yes."

"But why does he want them? And why turn them into monsters?"

He thought she'd fallen asleep, for she closed her eyes, but a moment later, she said, "Pride? Vanity? Maybe he does it just to hurt me. They'd be more mine than his if they stayed like this, and he hates to share anything, let alone something so precious." She cupped the back of the baby's head to squeeze him tighter against her. "I've often wondered what would happen if he left them alone, though. Would they mature into men? Could they have a normal life?"

"Perhaps 'tis best not to know," Eoin mumbled.

"Perhaps."

"After they've been…changed, do they remember? That you're their…?"

"Mother? There are times I'm certain they must; when they vie for my attention and purr like great cats whilst I pet them. And they let you live when I asked it of them, even though they resented doing so. But other times, I believe they'd kill me if they could. Especially the eldest. He so reminds me of his father. He scares me."

They fell to thinking. The day was not yet done, but driving rain blotted out the sky, and inside the cottage, they were outside of time. It felt as though they'd touched upon that charmed twilit hour when secrets were easiest to share.

"'Tis my doing," she confessed hastily so as not to lose her nerve. "I was young then, far too young. I didn't love him as I've learned to love the others."

"I wouldn't blame you even if that were true, but it isn't. Through your compassionate nature, I can gauge the breadth of your heart. I doubt it has ever been found wanting."

The shadow of a smile skimmed across her lips. "Still an awful tease."

"No, Cinnia. Trust me when I say that I have never seen such grace nor such goodness as I have in you. In all the world, there isn't another woman, or man for that matter, who has given so freely and sacrificed so much. You are beautiful, Cinnia, the most beautiful soul I've…"

Some colour was restored to her cheeks. Eoin grew shy

and focused on the stew bubbling in the cooking pot. If it could be considered stew. With the amount of water they had added to stretch what meagre scraps were left, it would've been generous to call it broth. Nevertheless, it was nice to curl his hands around a bowlful and have its warmth seep into his fingers. He breathed of it as deeply as Cinnia did her child, luxuriating in its heat, before offering the bowl to her.

He wasn't surprised when she refused. The babe had only just settled, she reasoned, and besides this, Eoin needed to eat just as much as she did, and really, she wasn't all that hungry anyway, and so on and so forth until Eoin stopped listening to consider the possibility that a compassionate nature in excess might be as troublesome as when in short supply.

To spare them both from this exercise in patience, Eoin pried the baby from her arms and presented the bowl in exchange.

"Drink," he said, ignoring her objections, and then set about quietening the affronted child. It seemed a dance of sorts, and he was a quick study in its steps. A jiggle here, a pat there, and the squalling softened to hiccups. Eoin grinned. There was something in the way the tiny wee mite relaxed against his chest that was profoundly rewarding.

"There's a good lad. He needs a name, I think."

"No, he doesn't." She watched them over the brim of the bowl. "Remember what I've told you."

"He isn't mine to love," Eoin recited, properly chastised.

The threat of overwhelming despair descended, but Eoin beat it back. He wouldn't increase Cinnia's burden any more than he already had, choosing instead to lessen it however he could. Although the fire crackled gaily, lighting the room with a mellow orange glow, it didn't keep out the damp, and he eyed the holes in the thatching through which the rain snuck inside. He'd see to that in short order, though there were more pressing issues to attend to first.

"When this bedeviling rain stops, I'll away to the village and bring back so much food your cupboard won't be able to hold it all."

"That isn't necessary."

Eoin looked at her sideways.

"I've always had enough to survive," she said. "The Beast enjoys his games and won't stand to see them spoiled. I'm not allowed any manner of escape, least of all death. Besides…" She stared down into the bowl as if reading a fortune. "When you leave here, you are never to return."

They had argued this same point throughout the day. Regardless of the path their conversation took, always they circled round to this. Luckily, his charge chose this moment to let out a squeaking yawn.

"What was that, hey, little man? What did you say?"

"Eoin…"

"A right smart little man you are. Yes, you are."

"Eoin, give him to me. Now."

Wordlessly, he handed her the baby. He kept his back to them as he refilled the emptied bowl. The healing herbs she'd instructed him to crumble into the stew lent it a bitter taste, yet he savoured it anyway because it served as another distraction. He wasn't going to speak to her until she spoke of something other than his leaving. Because he wasn't going to leave. Not ever.

"Don't," Cinnia said.

"Don't what?"

"Scheme. Plot."

He blinked at her, feigning innocence.

She sighed. "You could plan for a thousand years and still wouldn't win against him."

"I might," he replied, needled into a child-like sulk.

"Eoin, please. You have to go. Should you stay much longer, he—"

"Am I really to accept this? Am I to abandon you to his grotesque lust? I won't go! I won't! I'd rather die!"

"But I would rather you live. I want you as far from here as possible so that I'll know you're safe and can imagine the pretty life you lead. I will picture you in a house by the sea," she mused, smiling faintly. "I've always dreamt of the sea. It sounds glorious. All that water... So then, a little house. A little garden full of flowers, and fat, merry children at your feet. Oh, won't you describe your Muireann, that I might better imagine her beside you?"

He scowled at the fire. He didn't wish to talk of anything, much less Muireann. She wasn't even real to him anymore. Nothing was.

"My life is yours, Cinnia," he grumbled to the flames at length. "I'm honour bound to obey you. And that's what I do. I obey." He paused to steady himself, to force rising anger back down where it belonged. "But tell me, how am I to imagine you? Will not the cruellest parts of my mind remind me that you're either screaming in pain or crying without comfort? There are no 'pretty' stories on which I can rely. You shall haunt me to my death."

Outside, the rain picked up its pace, and the trees groaned under its weight. The clatter of all that merciless weather hammering down on the roof was deafening, but even so, Eoin caught the subtle change in Cinnia's breathing. He had made her cry! He immediately threw himself beside her, begging she forgive him his petulance.

"She has hair like honey, my Muireann," he then whispered against the top of her head. "She is sloe-eyed, freckled, and sweet. She is the Queen of a castle made of stone white as milk, and from its walls, you can see the ocean stretching on for miles and miles, perfect and endless and pure. It glitters as gold when the sun is high. Otherwise, it changes from blue to green to grey. There are cliffs of blackest rock all around, and the grass grows thick and wild."

Sniffling, she nuzzled into him. "And the flowers?"

"There are flowers everywhere you look, Cinnia. They bloom in countless colours, small as a dewdrop or with petals larger than my hand. They dance in the wind and call all creatures to join them. Bees drowsy with nectar. Butterflies whose wings the fairies envy. Birds too. There are so many birds. The sky is filled with song."

He went on, conjuring every bit of beauty he'd ever seen, holding her and her doomed baby safe within his arms, until she drifted off. *If only I could always do this for her,* he thought, watching her sleep, for there had never been a feat of strength nor an act of bravery that felt so close to the heart of what it meant to be a man.

CHAPTER 9

reams, though harried, defended Eoin from a multitude of troubles, but this reprieve was short-lived. Upon awakening to another tediously cheerless dawn, he had to confront his injuries all over again. His eyes burned. Bells clanged in his ears. He tasted copper in his mouth and bile at the back of his throat. Every movement he made, however slight, produced visceral, screaming protest. Even so, he refused to indulge in self-pity.

Sitting up to roll out his whinging shoulders, he noticed Cinnia was no longer in bed beside him. He called her name. She didn't answer. For a moment, with his mind still clouded by sleep and preoccupied with pain, he didn't think much of this. Then it occurred to him, what her absence must mean, and dread washed everything else away.

He shot out from the cottage, but a perilous excess of mud plotted against him. His legs sprawled in different directions, just like that of a fresh lamb. He slowed to gain traction, which meant reason had time enough to commandeer his mind, and reason showed no mercy. It told him to reject the assurances of pride, for pride mistook strength of desire for ability. He'd no hope of defeating the Beast, regardless of how he wished otherwise. Cinnia would be the one to suffer should he rush headlong to her side. Her son, he realised, heart sinking, must already be lost.

Bodily pain was nothing to him then, not when weighed against the absolute, soul-crushing torment that had him teetering on his heels and tearing at his hair. His mouth moved silently, but ere long he began to moan and then to wail. Finally, he bellowed as a rabid bull. He'd never been a man known for wanton violence, yet he craved nothing more in that instant than to kill. Anything. Anyone.

There came a rustling to the east of the clearing. He spun around, ready for a fight, his fists achingly tight. A crazed grin stretched his lips as he watched a man emerge from the wooden labyrinth.

The stranger was a doddering old tramp. Rheumy eyes peered out from behind a beard matted with filth, and he didn't breathe so much as gargle phlegm. Though Eoin's grin lost none of its choler, it faltered. This wretch was hardly a worthy opponent. He sneered to show his disappointment. In fear, the man scuttled back so quickly that the mud had its way with his feet. He careened to and fro, arms spiralling, and were it not for the basket strapped to his humped back acting as a counterweight, he'd have fallen over.

Once he recovered his balance, he set the basket down while rattling out a great sigh, resigning himself to whatever barbarism he imagined Eoin would inflict upon him. Then there passed a glimmer of recognition across the wizened face. It gave him courage enough to speak.

"I took you for dead, Sir Knight. From the look of you, I'm only half wrong."

Eoin eyed him with renewed curiosity, though his memory was a muddle. It was only when the old man smiled that Eoin could place him.

"The beggar from the village?"

"Turlough, they call me."

"What business have you here?"

"Food. For the witch."

"Witch," Eoin repeated softly. He said it again, posing it as a question, offering the man a chance to recant the slur, but nothing more than a dull stare met this gesture of goodwill, and so his blood rapidly returned to a boil. "*Witch*?!" he howled, much to Turlough's fright. "You dare?! By the gods, you shall pay for your gall!"

Eoin lunged, seizing him by the neck. Turlough made a noise not unlike the croaking of a raven and managed little in the way of resistance. There was no challenge in throttling the enfeebled, yet satisfaction tingled up Eoin's arms regardless. It was on this bastard's counsel that Eoin had mistreated Cinnia after all. It was because he professed her evil that Eoin had done the same. He wasn't worth even one of her tears but had been the cause of far too many.

Eoin wanted to tell Turlough all that had happened. He ought to die knowing the full extent of his sins, yet it was as though Eoin were the one strangled, so powerless was he to speak. Instead, he cackled and growled and even sobbed. His grip tightened. As it did, his sight blurred so he couldn't see the bulging tongue or the bluing face. He saw only his own guilt, his own puerile readiness to condemn an innocent woman. Witch, Eoin had called her, time after time, though she was the greatest hero the world had yet known.

"Stop."

Cinnia sailed through the trees. She was stately and splendid despite her poor, tired eyes and sunken cheeks. Eoin dropped Turlough without a care as to how he retched. His wrath didn't allow for pity, and only when he had Cinnia in his arms did the madness abate. She graciously accepted the embrace, but when he tried to ask after her son, she silenced him with one acidic look.

"You are late this month," she said, as she moved to stand over Turlough. "I've warned you not to make a habit of this and will not warn you again."

Turlough couldn't find air enough to answer, although Eoin doubted he'd have apologised if he could. Cinnia observed him with the same haughty disinterest she'd shown

Eoin upon their first meeting, with cold-blooded intellect flashing forth just as brilliantly as it had then. She was acquainted with the man, this much was clear, which meant he'd known of her plight all along and still chose to sully her name.

Dark wings beat about Eoin's head. He stomped to the basket Turlough had brought. Inside there were little sacks of grain, a chunk of hard cheese, meagre cuts of salted ox-flesh and mutton, and a dollop of lard. There were various greens and roots too, though they were fit for nought but swine.

"This is meant to last the month? Why, there's less than a fortnight's worth! It isn't enough she's a slave to the Beast, she should starve too? And this hovel," he said, gesturing wildly. "This beggarly collection of twigs and rock she's forced to live in, is this your doing?"

"'Tis more than she deserves," came the sour reply.

Cinnia threw herself in Eoin's path, and with good reason. He was now more of a beast himself than a man, quite beyond compassion. He'd have ripped Turlough limb from limb had he been able, yet, inexplicably, Turlough didn't escape while he had the chance. He muttered that Eoin was bewitched, that Cinnia was a brazen whore. Enough talk! Eoin would wring the life from Turlough as slowly as he could to prolong the pain. It would be his first attempt at torture, but he was keen to learn.

However, much as he tried, Eoin couldn't get to him. Not without knocking Cinnia aside, and this, naturally, was unthinkable. So he pleaded for permission to defend her honour, hoping the frustration reddening his skin would persuade her to agree.

She shook her head. "You won't become a murderer for my sake."

"But I am one already! I'm a weapon born to be wielded!"

"Can you not see she's fashioned you into her fool?" Turlough jeered. "That's what she does. She seduces good men towards sin."

"She saved me, as she has saved us all!"

"You deserve a cleaner end than this, my son. I'd steer you into death straightaway were I able."

"By all means, go ahead and try, you daft, hedge-born cad!"

"Enough," said Cinnia. "This is my home. I would have peace."

Her jaw was taut, her brow stern, and although her mouth remained soft, it was pensive rather than inviting. She could have sat upon any throne in any kingdom in any age and wouldn't have appeared out of place. Were his life not already hers, Eoin would pledge it to her at once. As it was, with only obedience left to offer, he swallowed his anger and awaited her next command.

Trusting Eoin wouldn't attack, she released him. To Turlough, she said, "Go. I grow weary of your spiteful nonsense."

"I pray the day never comes that you do not hear the creak of your mother's noose."

"Charming."

Turlough made to leave but then hesitated. Stooping, he grasped the basket of food and turned its contents out into the mud. Eoin wasn't aware he was in motion until Cinnia stopped him. The old man built himself into a seething, sputtering rage, pointing accusingly at their entwined hands. Curses spewed from his frothing mouth with the speed and force of a fatal disease. Cinnia only tightened her hold on Eoin. Even now, she wouldn't permit him to exact any revenge on her behalf.

"His words are nothing, as he is nothing. Pay him no mind."

"Had you even a whiff of shame, you'd release this poor man, but I reckon a witch has no shame to spare."

She bristled in spite of her own advice. "And had *you* any sense, you wouldn't try my patience further."

"Do you think me scared of you, witch?"

"I think you should be. Need I remind you of the price your son paid for his disrespect?"

"How dare you!"

"Perhaps if you'd raised a man instead of a pig, Arlyn would still be alive. But maybe I should thank you. I had nearly two whole days to myself while my master and Arlyn played together."

Bleating out a garbled war cry, Turlough scratched at the

air and reached for Cinnia's neck. Eoin hadn't the chance to react before a screeching blur burst forth from the trees. Suddenly, the old man was on his back, weakly pushing against a pebbled snout. Though the snout was small, the smallest Eoin had yet seen, its teeth were sharp. They made quick work of Turlough's tender throat. The babe, so newly born and so recently transformed, chirped at his mother, quite proud of himself.

But then both he and Eoin discovered why ragged flesh and pooling blood hadn't tempted his brothers from the shade. The sky was awash with clouds, the sun well-hidden behind them, but as a creature of darkness and such a young one at that, he had no defence against the light of day. Still-soft scales began to smoke. Eyes bulged in frantic confusion as pure white flames consumed them. A high-pitched scream trailed off into moans.

Compelled by emotion more paternal than any he'd ever known, Eoin held him as he died. The tiny hand tipped with tiny claws curled around Eoin's finger once again. Cinnia crowded close and sang.

Sleep now and dream, dear
The fairies are calling
Can you not hear the songs that they sing?

Sail over seas made of stardust and moonbeams
Fly across skies made of gold
To a lullaby land

Where the fairies are waiting
Join them in dance upon the green wold

"There's a good lad," Eoin whispered, as the jerking slowed to a stop. "There's a brave boy."

Cinnia bent to place one last kiss upon his head, right between the budding horns. Eoin did the same. It was effortless for him now, to look beyond the monster and see the child.

"They *do* remember," he said, more to himself than to Cinnia. "He protected you. He loved you."

"And he is dead," she replied listlessly. "Such is the price of love."

CHAPTER 10

hey didn't speak. That which went unsaid simmered in the air until silence alchemised into staggering oppression. It crushed down on them, as it had in those first days Eoin spent in Cinnia's care, as he imagined it had in all the days that came before. *This isn't living*, he decided sadly. This was merely the last breath before death, stretched out and spread thin. They were frozen. Fixed in time. Forced to inhabit the same terrible moment of hopelessness for all eternity.

The babe had been laid to rest in the hollow of a leaning elm. They made for him a bed of dark green needles and swaddled him in blankets of moss, and when they were done, it looked as though he'd always belonged to the tree. Soon enough, he would, and Eoin prayed this would grant the boy's poor wee soul some peace. He hated to think of it blundering about in a furious fog like the other ghosts or, even worse, that it was lost and afraid and crying for its mother.

Back at the cottage, Eoin and Cinnia gathered up the spilt food to wipe it clean as best they could. Neither remarked upon the taste of dirt while they ate a meal of oatcakes and thinned stew. They slept a little, stared off into nothing a little, slept a bit more. Wood creaked. Water dripped. The fire popped and spat. And they did not speak.

It was then that Cinnia heard her master's call. She shook her head when Eoin moved to follow her, and he was left behind with only bitter thoughts for company.

Outside, Turlough's corpse languished in the mud. Cinnia hadn't needed to say what to do with this body because her remaining children clearly intended to dispose of it themselves come nightfall. Eoin heard them chittering impatiently to one another and watched for the sparkle of eyes hidden amongst shifting leaves. Then for reasons unknown and unsought, he spoke to them.

"Hungry, are you, lads? Surely you must fancy sweeter meat than this tough old bag of bones."

They responded as he supposed they might. All conversation ceased, and they didn't move except, he guessed, to crane their long necks forward so as not to miss a word.

"You showed great restraint not to kill me when by all rights, my life was yours. If not for the sun, would you claim me as your prize?"

No reply. On another incomprehensible whim, Eoin took hold of Turlough by the ankles. It was a simple task to drag him closer to the trees, so light was he despite the rigid weight of death. When shadows danced upon the old man's face, Eoin stepped back, and something more paw than hand snaked around a tree trunk to sink its claws into the pallid skin. Turlough's head dashed against the roots as he was wrenched into darkness.

"Now, now, you mustn't fight," Eoin said in answer to sudden snarling.

If they'd listened to him before, they didn't do so now. Their wooded haven shook with the bedlam of battle. Branches cracked and crashed to the ground, raining bark, leaves, and a rubied splatter. Blood. Eoin bent to touch it. Still warm. *Not from Turlough then.* Why did this trouble him? He rubbed it between his fingers whilst the presumed victor bounded away with the others in feverish pursuit. They disappeared into the thick of the forest, and Eoin straightened, kicked dirt over the little puddle of blood, and waited as if in a trance for Cinnia's return.

She limped back into the yard a short while later. Her lip was swollen to the point of splitting. Scratches, angry and oozing, encircled her neck. "You will leave at dawn," she declared, rejecting Eoin's outstretched arms.

He saw in her a severity that would brook no argument, so he offered none. It wasn't until late in the night, when a lonely wind whistled over the roof, that Eoin dared breach the void.

"Cinnia, do you think life schools the boy to shape the

man?"

Though she tried to remain aloof, curiosity softened her resolve.

"My mother once told me we are all but parts of a tree," he said, encouraged. "As she explained it, we are like roots or sap or bark, working together towards a common goal. To ensure we won't lessen the whole, the quality of our character is tested by the gods throughout our lives."

Cinnia frowned but waited for him to continue.

"I believed her. I lived by her words. Yet lately I fear… Was she wrong? A tree may be made of many parts, yet one that cannibalises itself cannot flourish. Or if it can, then should it?" He sighed deeply. "Ah, you must forgive me. My mind is restless. The fault is mine, I expect, for never seeking to tame it."

"What do you mean?" she asked, now thoroughly engrossed.

"Permitting others to think for me has ever been my habit. More than habit really. Duty." The intensity of his resentment shocked him, but he didn't try to suppress it. "I am a weapon. I am supposed to serve my betters faithfully and without question. That is my contribution to the tree. That is to say, it was. Until…"

"Until?"

"I chose to fight the Beast. 'Twas selfish desire, not duty, which brought me here. I abandoned all I'd been taught, everything that I was, in the reckless hope of becoming someone I'm not."

He was lost to memory then, picturing Muireann at the moment the world changed. Cold stone had dwarfed her as she perched on the throne that belonged to her father. She had smiled at Eoin, although now he recalled just how mournful a smile it was. It hadn't always been so. Once it was the stuff of sunshine, and he'd been chasing after its warmth ever since.

He tapped his forehead. "I live in here. In fantasies better left to children. I imagine for myself glory and riches. And love," he added, finally conceding that years had passed since Muireann last bestowed her favour upon him. "I try on different lives and discard them as I please. You do this too, don't you?"

She nodded. "I should go mad otherwise."

"Yet such a life, one lived between blind obedience and untried fancy cripples one's reasoning. I am ill-prepared for the crossroads I face. Do I continue to serve the tree?"

Or do I bring an axe to it?

"Cinnia," he said, looking to her in a state of helplessness, "I am undone."

This wasn't right. She'd shouldered so much for so long. For her sake, he ought to conceal all that devilled him. The erstwhile stories he'd told her, he should tell again, but they seared his tongue and tasted of ashes. When Cinnia drew his head upon her lap, he could have wept with relief despite how awful it was to steal more strength from her.

"And now you must forgive me," she softly said, "for 'tis *my* selfish desire that has brought you so low. I did not save you from my sons out of the goodness of my heart, Eoin. That day we met, you were kind to me. You didn't have to be, but you were, and I hadn't seen anything of kindness since my mother died. I wanted—*needed*—more of it. Because if I could pretend that someone like you were mine, even for a little while, then I could also pretend I was someone worthy of respect and of...of love. I'd be a woman for once and not a witch. Oh, I knew you'd see through my lies eventually and that it would end poorly for the both of us, but I just had to try on a different life, as you've put it."

She thought *she* was selfish? That *he* was kind? He'd have laughed at how absurd this was if it also weren't so intolerably sad. He had been cold, his words crude. Only someone who'd lived an uncommonly mean life would mistake his lack of further aggression for kindness. He said this to her and then taking her hands, he kissed them. "Dearest lady, you are not a witch, and you owe me no apologies."

"I am, and I do!" she cried. "I've used you horribly. That you suffer so badly is due to my weakness, not yours."

"I beg you, stop. You are my saviour. Better still, you are my friend, and for this, I am glad."

Her eyes misted, but she shook free of his hands and went to busy herself at her cupboard, her back to him, shoulders tense. The walls Eoin had pulled apart were rising once more. This was how she survived before him. This was how she would survive when he was gone. But he couldn't let her shut him out just yet. If these were to be their final hours together, he wouldn't squander them.

"I cannot begin to tell you how much I ad—"

She hurried to interrupt. "I have two things to ask of you."

"Of course. I'll do whatever you wish."

"First, swear to me that you won't waste the chance I've given you. You are to live. More than this, you are to live well. Return to Muireann's side, and with her love banish all thought of the evil you've uncovered here." When he didn't answer, she turned to fix him with a wintry stare. "Well? Eoin, will you swear it?"

"No."

She scowled. "Why not?"

"I can only swear to that which is within my control."

"What are you saying?"

"That Muireann does not love me."

"But she must!"

"She might have. When we were children. She doesn't anymore."

"Oh. Oh, I see." Cinnia gazed at him over licks of fire, her face brimming with a maudlin pity that brought heat to his own. "You came here to win her heart?"

He held her eyes for as long as he could, but the

humiliation of it all was overwhelming. He looked away.

"There's no hope?" she murmured.

"None."

She began to say one thing and then stopped to say another, her manner decidedly indignant. Her hands flew to her hips as she said, "You are young and handsome and good. You will choose another, someone more deserving of your affection, and that stupid, *stupid* girl will rue her loss."

Eoin very nearly smiled.

"So then, with that in mind, will you swear to wed someone whose love will console you in those times you need it most?"

He agreed that if it would make her happy, he'd endeavour to find such a woman. He didn't confess that this notion held little appeal, but she could probably read that in the wrinkling of his brow. Still, she seemed mollified. Then coming to sit on the edge of the bed, she held out her hands. He accepted them at once, kissed them just as he'd done minutes before, and played with her fingers, marvelling at how deceptively delicate they felt compared to his. He also hoped this would make her forget about her second request because he suspected that he'd hate it even more than the first. However, she was too clever for his tricks. Twisting at the wrists, she switched the position of their hands so that she kept his from wandering.

"Now this is very important, Eoin, so please hear me out," she said, then chewed on her lip and said nothing more until he grudgingly nodded. "If ever you speak of me, you must swear to speak instead of the witch, of the demon's whore, and not of the martyr you believe me to be."

He rolled his eyes. "I could never—"

"You must! In the beginning, you doubted me, didn't you? You thought me wicked."

"I was wrong."

"No, you were only too right. Listen to me," she shouted above Eoin's rising protests. To stop him from storming off, she tightened her hold on him. "I wasn't chosen for beauty alone. The Beast could have had a hundred beauties, nay, a thousand if he so desired. He chose me for the frailty he saw in me, for the flaw he could further corrupt."

"I don't believe it. I won't! Cinnia, you have the gentlest, the sweetest, the best of hearts!"

Tossing her hair dismissively, she rose. She circled the fire, head bowed as if in prayer. But she did not pray. She remembered.

"When he came for me, I was told to be brave," she whispered. "That the world would be saved if I satisfied him. But they didn't tell me what that would entail. I thought he meant to devour me. I was only a child; I didn't know the ways of men. That first night, I…"

Eoin moved to comfort her, but she recoiled so violently at his touch that he dared not try again.

"Afterwards, I ran. I made it as far as the village." She fell upon her chair, her eyes dark with shadows. "These were my kinsmen. The people I had loved since birth. I was sure of their help. Yet, to them, one child was a fair price to end the slaughter. When they saw me, they went wild with anger and set about beating me with sticks, chasing me back to where he waited."

"Villains," said Eoin, disgusted.

She offered a half-hearted shrug. "Their choice was one of two horrors, and they chose what was for them the lesser. They hate me for it, though."

"They hate themselves," he corrected, beginning to understand why they cursed she whom they ought to have deified. "They believed selling you to the Beast would save them, but, Cinnia, you should see how they live. Their sin has reduced them to savages. They feel no joy, no sense of peace. They are as the wraiths haunting this forest, and they call you a witch out of desperation to forget that they did this to themselves."

"Did they? I'll admit there is a part of me that's delighted to hear of their suffering, but are they really to blame? You don't know what it was like back then. You didn't see the destruction, the death."

"I can imagine it."

"No, you can't," she said wearily. "Be grateful for that."

"No. They should have let the world burn instead. I would have. I would never have willingly given anyone to that bastard, let alone a child." He glowered at the fire, only looking up again when he heard Cinnia's faint chuckle. She was watching him with fondness and with regret, and he realised what he'd just said. "I didn't mean that! I'm so sorry, I wasn't thinking, I—"

"Shhh, worry not. Perhaps you'll be able to keep that second promise to me after all, so long as you remember that I too have bargained with the devil. It happened on that very first night. As punishment for running away, I learned what it was that the Beast wanted most. If I'd been strong like you, bold enough to die for what was right, I would have refused. But I was young and afraid. And weak. So I agreed. I bore him a son to save my own wretched skin. Don't," she snapped before Eoin could say a word. "Don't try to excuse what I've done. I'm no fool. I knew even then that I made the wrong choice. I swore never to make it again, yet I've since broken that vow many times over.

"Not for myself, of course. My life lost its value years ago. And not even for those lecherous men, Arlyn and the rest, who are drawn here like flies to honey and delude themselves into thinking they can have me for their own. These men my master kills, and good riddance to them, but he tells me their blood awakens old appetites. With the gift of a son, I can persuade him to return to the earth and sleep. And sleep he must, if the world is to survive."

"There, you see, that is the epitome of bravery! Of

unmatched heroism!"

"Is it? You brand those who gave him one child villains. I've now given him seven! Seven sons, seven souls forced to become monsters. They didn't ask for this life any more than I did. And when…"

She scrubbed a hand over her face and left it there, thumb rubbing circles onto her temple. Eoin waited for her to gather her courage. It took quite some time.

"When my beauty fades," she tentatively began, "and he finds himself in want of softer, sweeter flesh, he will ask for a daughter to take my place. I will give him one. Even knowing the torture she'll endure, I will. Do you still think me heroic?"

His conviction waned, yet he clung to it anyway. "You have no choice."

"Yes, I do. I have always had a choice, and I choose to sacrifice my children before their very conception. My mother killed herself the day I was wed to the Beast. She couldn't bear it. But I can. And I do."

He didn't know what to say and stood gaping at her like a simpleton. Her lips curled in a wry smile. She explored his eyes and gave another shrug to whatever it was she saw in them.

"I love my children, Eoin, but that doesn't stop me from hurting them. I am as much a monster as the Beast. Worse, I should think, as I'm capable of guilt while he is not. So you will go from here, and you won't speak of my beauty or my heart or my sorry circumstances. You will call me a witch and mean every word. Because if you don't and others come in search of me, the lives I'll have to destroy will be on your head just as much as they are on mine."

The flickering of flames stole her attention. She reached out a hand to them, holding it so close that soot darkened her palm. If this brought her pain, she showed no sign of it. She seemed to him then not a woman nor even a witch but an empty shell.

"You will leave at dawn."

CHAPTER 11

ust as the starless night traded black for dusty grey, the Beast summoned Cinnia to his lair. He meant to keep them apart, Eoin guessed. He wouldn't give them time to linger over their goodbyes. Cinnia was right. The means with which he inflicted pain were limitless.

Was it time for a final show of rebellion? If Eoin remained while dawn came and went, would he have to forfeit the life Cinnia had bought for him? That was hardly a deterrent. Quite the opposite really. But no. He wouldn't test the patience of the Beast. He couldn't. Cinnia wanted Eoin to live, so he would live. She wanted him to go, so he would go. This was her wish. He had to respect it and leave her to her duty and her inconceivably appalling fate.

Standing in the doorway of her cottage, Eoin could almost see her huddled next to the fire, sobbing and bleeding. A growl escaped his throat. And then another. He couldn't contain them, didn't bother to try. Hatred spread like a festering wound. He let loose a scream. At first, it was just fury forced into sound. Then little by little, it shaped itself into a singular word, which he drew out for as long as his lungs permitted.

"Why?!"

The lurking ghosts gave no answer. Eoin asked them again, for surely they had some sort of insight that could make sense of this senselessness. But maybe death halved their souls, reduced them to the most elementary of emotions. Did they watch him so keenly only because he possessed that which they coveted? Had everything but greed been stripped away from them?

His stomach sank. He was now more like the dead than he was himself. He yearned just as they yearned, pined as they pined. Need that would never be sated bored a hole down to his heart and all he used to be drained away through it. He was cursed. Had to be. Why else would the dead want so badly to count him amongst their numbers?

"Go away," he bellowed. "Leave me alone!"

And for a moment, they complied. The pressure of their spectral eyes abated. His chest emptied in an appreciative whoosh, but the respite was short-lived. Something else took over the vigil in their stead. He knew it from the way his hair stood on end. Yet Eoin was unafraid. He was wary, yes, anxious even, but not afraid. Butterflies of anticipation swarmed into that which had been hollowed out. He turned to the direction he most felt their presence with arms spread wide and a manic gleam in his eye.

"What are you waiting for?" he shouted to Cinnia's sons. "Here I am. Alone. Unarmed. Unable to fight even half as well as I did before." He tugged the neck of his shirt, exposing his ravaged shoulder. "Look here. See how deeply you've marked me? When it rains, when the cold sets in, this joint will trouble me as if it belongs to a man of fifty." He pushed up his sleeves. "And here too. The scars are yet red, but in time, they'll look as though you've sewn threads of moonlight into my skin. More reminders that I am weak where you are strong and lost where you have won."

Grasping at a low hanging branch, his foot on a root, he peered around a tree where he thought one of them hid, but they sped away before he caught sight of them.

"Why do you run? The sun still sleeps, and I won't resist."

The undergrowth crunched. He spun around. Nothing. He followed the noise anyway, ducking under draping vines, climbing over rotting logs. It was darker here. He had to squint to see, but that only added to the thrill.

Was he the hunter or the hunted?

Did it matter?

"Your mother asked you to spare me," he said to a grove where the shadows collected and fog smothered the ground in dense grey sheets. "But your mother isn't here now, so surely this is a perfect time to finish what you started. When she finds the cottage empty, she'll just assume I've gone away."

There was a flash of movement, albeit brief. Eoin's gaze fixed upon a piece of mottled brown bone half-hidden beneath a pile of mouldering cloth. It was a skull. Most of one anyway. On bended knee, he idly examined it with a feather-light touch. There, the socket that once held an eye. The triangle that had been a nose. What sort of man was he? What dreams had he held closest to his heart? Had he begged for his life, or did he offer it up as freely as Eoin did now?

He cleared his throat. "Shall I tell you a story? There once was a girl. Muireann was her name. She was the daughter of the King and, as the only one of his children to survive infancy, heir to the crown. The people adored her. She was pampered and protected, raised by a veritable army of nursemaids who shielded her from as much of the world's ugliness as they could."

A twig snapped. In his periphery, Eoin spied something the colour of rust creeping towards him. Madness bubbled up from the pit of his stomach, yet still, there was no fear. The sensation was unfamiliar, intoxicating. He hummed absentmindedly in an excitement just shy of pleasure before continuing.

"One day, I'm not sure how, she slipped away from her watchers. She'd a fondness for the hounds and had a notion to visit them. These were not pets, though. They were warriors in their own right and, like you, they craved the taste of blood.

Muireann didn't understand this. She'd been tricked by their silly grins and wagging tails. When she went to see them, she thoughtlessly brought with her a wee fox that was a gift from her father. I tried to hurry her away, but the fox leapt free and made to run. Well, you know those dogs were on it before I could stop them."

The creature inched closer. Eoin sat back upon his heels, palms resting on his thighs. He didn't want to die, not really, but neither did the idea of death concern him anymore.

"Muireann was beside herself. She demanded I punish the hounds. I consoled her as best I could, but I was just a boy. I think I wasn't as considerate to her feelings as I could have been."

He glanced over his shoulder. The creature was barely a foot away from him. It was only the size of a yearling goat, but each of its claws was the length of a dagger. When their eyes met, it displayed the crowding of its teeth. Lightning coursed through Eoin's limbs. Slowly, he shifted his weight and turned to it, still crouched.

"Do you know what I told her? I said, 'Why, Princess, don't you see? 'Tis but the nature of the beast.'"

His legs went weak from his explosion of laughter. He flopped down onto his backside, and the creature jumped in surprise. He was vaguely aware of motion beside him, behind him, above him. Footsteps snuck in on all sides. Finally, *finally*, fear pricked his spine and slid along his scalp. But there was nothing for it now. He relaxed the involuntary clenching of his jaw.

"Good lads. Truly, 'tis a kindness you do me. I cannot leave her, no matter the promises I made." To the heavens, he said, "If ever there was a god who loved me, I prithee you hear me now. Let me stay with Cinnia. Let me always watch over her. In death, let me somehow comfort her as I couldn't in life."

Then, shutting his eyes, he waited. The rustling grew louder. Sour breath puffed against his chest, and although he still felt the pain from the strength of their bite, he bared his neck. Would it be quick, or would they make a game of it? His pulse rabbited. Blood raged as a flooded river through his ears, and sweat beaded across his tingling skin.

When contact was suddenly made, he gasped. The creature was as hard as a rock, yet warm. It pushed and pushed until it lifted Eoin's hand, and then this nightmare made of rape and fire eschewed the ghoulish purpose for which it was bred. It nuzzled into Eoin's side just as another laid its heavy head upon his lap and a third placed a paw onto his leg. They purred as cats, Cinnia had said, and Eoin learned this to be true. He opened his eyes on a smile.

A wistful, drowsy calm descended as Eoin settled into the unlikely truce. He hummed a melody from boyhood to an appreciative audience, though his voice was rough as their hide.

Tracing the patterns made by their scales, his fingertips danced along grooves and over bumps and ridges. The creatures melted under his touch, stretching, sighing, smacking their mouths, content to let him lavish them with affection. The only interruption to their happy rumbling came when one or another tried to steal all the petting for themselves, but Eoin had only to say, "Hush now," in order to quell the squawking complaints.

They listen, he thought in amazement. *They learn.*

Yet one amongst them refused to be coddled. This child, the eldest, the one who frightened Cinnia, sat some distance apart with resentment bunching up its leathered muzzle. It was arrogant and so full of anger that Eoin shivered whenever he glanced its way. He suspected even the slightest provocation would cause the spiteful thing to attack. He was fortunate then, to have spent many years in the company of war hounds. He knew to keep his movements slow and his gaze soft.

"Your mother says you've no need of names," he began, smiling without showing teeth. "She is wise, your mother, in every way I'm not, but in this, I believe her mistaken. Every man, whether high or lowborn, starts life with a name. I can't see why you should be any different. What say you? Would you like for me to give each of you names?"

They blinked up at him, eyes sparkling with something akin to that which he'd seen in the eyes of children receiving a trinket or toy. It was endearing and so at odds with the rest of their monstrous anatomy that Eoin's task was made all the more significant. He carefully regarded the creature nestled in the crook of his arm for some time before making his decision.

"You are Oisín," he declared and was rewarded with a cheery little chirrup. He turned to the next, sprawled further down his leg. "Hmm, who are you?" he teased, tapping his chin thoughtfully and chuckling at an impatient squeeze from a paw. "I have it! You are Cáelán." He smoothed his palm against the cheek of the one whom he'd blinded, saying, "I name you Ronan." Its head nudged up into his hand. Eoin gave it a scratch as he looked over the fourth child. "You, my boy, you shall be called Quillan. As for you, I can think of no other name better than Liadhnan," he finished, ending upon the one whose wings he'd torn. "I hope you will forgive me, Liadhnan, Ronan, for the harm I've done you. And certainly, lads, you likewise have *my* forgiveness. After all, we're friends now, aren't we?"

There was a bit of groaning and wiggling, which Eoin presumed to be agreement. He patted each one, repeating their newly dubbed names to them. There was no mistaking their boisterous gabbling for anything other than joy, but Eoin couldn't find it within himself to share in it because the eldest had yet to be named. Slowly, Eoin dragged his gaze up the length of this creature, noting the unnerving flex of its claws. He watched a growl roil through its neck and, for a second, he was sure he'd seen a flare of light just beneath the surface of its skin in the hollow of its throat.

"Áedgen," he whispered. *Born of fire.*

He swallowed thickly and tore his eyes away. The growling stopped. A name had appeased the boy to some extent, and perhaps if given enough time, Eoin could teach Áedgen how to control the anger churning within. However, time wasn't a luxury either had at their disposal. It was likely inevitable that each of the cursed children would grow more and more into the roles the Beast had designed for them, that of ruthless yet obedient soldiers, but while Eoin was here, while he had their attention, he would offer an alternative.

"If it pleases you, I should like to give my own name to your brother who sleeps nearby. I was there for his birth and his death, and I... I..."

He couldn't go on. How could he adequately explain what he was only starting to piece together himself? He drew in a shaking breath.

"Young Eoin was impossibly brave. He died as a man should die. Not for riches or glory or even for pride but for love. You can see the difference, can't you?" he asked, looking from one to the next. "Between what diminishes a man and what elevates him?"

They cocked their heads, curious and alert. Would that they could speak! While he was sure they understood his words, he had his doubts as to whether they understood his meaning.

"You are your *mother's* sons. Your hearts beat with *her* blood, and the names I've given you are a promise. Despite all that compels you otherwise, I beseech you to embrace that part of you which is wholly of her."

The back of his head thumped against wood. Frustration coiled around every fibre of his being like a colossal snake, its clasp ever tightening until he thought he should either suffocate or burst.

"What's to become of me?" he muttered to the stagnant air. "I tried to kill the Beast. I tried to kill myself. Yet I've failed at both. So what do I do now?"

Soft trilling coaxed from him a doleful smile. He glanced down into eyes that were so like Cinnia's that his chest ached. So human. Was it merely an illusion? How much of their souls burned away when they were cast into the fire?

Dawn broke. Eoin lifted his face towards it, though it was merely a whisper of what it ought to be. He sighed. Millennia felt to have passed since he last beheld a proper sky of blue and gold. Five of the children shuffled to avoid the weedy, dust-speckled beams of light that peeked through the gaps in the canopy. The sixth, Áedgen, sat unflinching and unafraid. Age had toughened his scales so that the sun didn't hurt him much, and as the shadows fell away from the cut and swell of each powerful muscle, he appeared even more daunting.

Eoin didn't shy from Áedgen's boastful stare. "If ever you think of me once I'm gone, I pray you will also remember this lesson. Strength means nothing if not used to protect those you love."

With that, he stood. He'd dawdled far too long and didn't want to think what this meant for Cinnia. For the third time, he repeated their names, ending on Áedgen to whom he gave a long, lingering look, wanting to see some sort of acknowledgement. He saw something else instead: a chink in Áedgen's impenetrable armour. Three small, diagonal slashes cut through the scales to the tender pink flesh beneath.

Eoin cried out, not from the discovery, but in response to that which fluttered to life within him. Scowling, Áedgen twisted his body to hide from Eoin's eager inspection. This did nothing to dissuade Eoin, as there were five other chances to confirm what he'd seen.

Yes, there. Across Cáelán's hind leg. And there on Liadhnan's back. Indeed, all had similar injuries in various stages of healing. Eoin knew at once what had made them. He'd been staring at such wounds upon his own body for weeks. He remembered the blood that splashed the ground during the fight for Turlough's corpse, and the thing fluttering inside him suddenly had a name.

Hope.

Forgetting all the King's hounds had taught him, he laughed in earnest, the force of which doubled him over. Those sons nearest to him were startled to their feet. They screeched, indignant, and some growled just as fiercely as

Áedgen, but that didn't concern Eoin in the least. Hope made him reckless. He revelled in it as a drunken god revels in wine.

"Don't worry, lads," he said, brushing tears of mirth from his cheek. "A pinch of madness is no cause for alarm."

His head swum with possibilities. But how to make them understand? More importantly, how to make them agree? Much as he relished this heady giddiness, he'd have to sober up to ensure they'd listen to him. He sucked his bottom lip between his teeth and weighed his options.

He didn't consider himself a particularly charismatic man. As the memory of crushed grass had always tempered his ambition, Eoin hadn't bothered to practice those sorts of impassioned speeches he'd heard so many times on the eve of battle. Nor had he studied the methods of men who, while either cowardly or infirm, garnered power using only cunning words woven together like a spell.

But he'd always been listening.

"I see myself in you. I too know how it feels to be torn between this," he tapped a finger on his forehead, "and this." He placed his palm over his heart. "'Tis the burden of sons born to callous and demanding fathers. We want so much to please them that we neglect our own desires. What a shame. Children shouldn't be forced down the same path as their father just because it suits his pride. They should be free to decide for themselves what they want and how best to leave their mark on the world."

Thus far, he'd managed to keep their interest. The smallest in particular, Oisín and Ronan, had gone slack-jawed with concentration. He gave each of their upturned snouts a friendly pat.

"When I look at you, at the gifts with which you've been blessed, I cannot help but imagine the exceptional lives you could lead. You are destined for greatness far beyond that of your father if only you refuse to lessen yourselves for the sake of his vanity."

Áedgen exhaled in what sounded suspiciously like his mother's scoff.

"You doubt me?" Eoin asked. "Small wonder. I suppose he's worked very hard to make you feel worthless and stupid and trapped."

He knelt before Áedgen and felt the rage billowing forth like steam. Eoin reached out his hand, hesitated, then steeled his nerve. He very slowly, very carefully caressed the stony curve of Áedgen's jaw. His hand trembled, but so did Áedgen's bravado.

"My poor, poor boy. What horrors have you seen?"

It was all too much for Áedgen. He jerked away, snapping his crooked fangs at Eoin's fingers. Eoin's pulse jumped. He blew out his cheeks to ease the throbbing in his chest and, standing, looked at the other children. They were as statues, their faces carved into lupine grimaces.

"I wish I could make him pay for all he's done. I would do

anything, give anything, to save you from him. I should have been able to… If he were but a man, I…" He stopped, breathless, and then tried again. "In the outside world, I am stronger than most, but here…" The browned skull caught his attention. He stooped to retrieve it. "Here, I am him. I am nothing."

Well, so be it, he thought, smashing the skull against a tree and letting the slivers slip through his fingers. *I have lived an unremarkable life, but I will make my death count for something.*

"I cannot grant you your freedom. No one can. There isn't a man alive who could end your father's reign. He's simply too strong. Yet for all that strength, he is weak. Aye, weak," he repeated to counter a scattering of incredulous squawks. "He's childish, brash, and so blinded by conceit that he hasn't noticed what you've become."

Eoin went back to Áedgen, kneeling just as before.

"He's used you to flatter himself, to pretend he's a god while he ruts in the rotting spoils of war. He doesn't love you. He thinks of you as his slaves, but, oh my sweet children, this is a lie. Look at yourselves. Look at the armour you wear, the weaponry you wield. These are not the bodies of slaves. You are princes, each of you. And if only you trust in me, I shall make you kings."

CHAPTER 12

craps of ruined leather caught Eoin's eye. A bracer. Squinting, he saw the faint outline of the family crest stamped upon it, and it reminded him of the life he'd once lived when authority was absolute and the world simple. He'd known only good and evil, virtue and vice. Nothing between. Nothing disguising itself as one when it was really the other.

"A root is a root," he mumbled. "A branch is a branch."

Because of its simplicity, his life had been one of relative ease. And yet he'd never been satisfied. He'd always suspected there must be some higher form of happiness that lay beyond the fetters of duty and guilt. Never had there been a time when that prospect hadn't whispered to him, effortlessly weaving itself into almost every thought he had, so that reality was constantly measured against fantasy, and thus was ever a disappointment.

The legion of restless dead marched in step behind him.

They'd no counsel to give, no strength they could lend. They were but echoes of himself, of his repressed desires and perceived failings. He would free them upon victory, or else join them in death, but in either event, they would trouble him no more after this day. He asked them to wait a little longer and walked on.

With a last look at the sky he wasn't likely to see again, he entered the lair of the Beast. Ashes drifted like snow, and smoke rushed forward to greet him. His lungs seized in protest. Uncontrollable coughing forced him to stop and allow his body time to adjust, but really, this was futile. It would only get worse the further down he went. He wiped his watering eyes on the back of his sleeve and walked on.

Conversation cut through the roar of hellfire. Cinnia's twittering soprano flew at speeds Eoin couldn't follow while the Beast's answering baritone rolled through rock, vibrating bits and pieces of precious metals, jingling them like thousands upon thousands of fairy bells. It was a final warning that if Eoin didn't turn back, he would cross over into a phantom realm from which he could never escape. But his choice was made, and he walked on.

The tunnel expanded. Eoin beat back the loathing that had settled over his skin and replaced it with something softer, something that spoke of deference and respect. It was with this guise that he faced the Beast.

He'd been expected. His foe reclined, in human form,

upon a golden hillock, the very picture of smug contentment. Cinnia was perched upon his lap, and though she didn't fight for freedom, the wicked arms encircling her waist constricted as if to remind them all to whom she belonged. She stared at Eoin, silent now except for those whimpers she couldn't control. He smiled at her sadly. There was still so much he wanted to say to her. He hoped she saw at least some of it in his eyes.

"So you've come again, little knight," the Beast said, interrupting their wordless exchange.

"I have."

"How amusing."

"Is it?"

"Indeed."

"Then perhaps you will consider indulging me."

The Beast sat up straighter. An impish light shone from the depths of his dark red eyes, a light so tainted by depravity that it raised the hair on the back of Eoin's neck. He didn't try to hide this. He gave in to his fear, letting it show quite clearly, and in response, a rough noise of approval rumbled in the Beast's chest.

"Go on," he whispered. "Tell me more."

"I wish to renew my challenge."

"Oh?"

"I won't rest until one of us is dead."

"Naturally," said the Beast, as Cinnia sobbed Eoin's name

into her hands. He wanted to look at her, to reassure her with the secret language of their eyes, but couldn't risk it.

"I ask you to fight me as you are now."

"Why is that, I wonder? Do you think it will improve your odds?"

"Not especially," Eoin sheepishly admitted.

The Beast laughed long and hard then pressed a smirk against Cinnia's ear. "I see why he stole your fancy. I've a mind to keep him for myself. We could have such fun."

"As is your right." Eoin drew nearer. "And once you defeat me, I'm prepared to submit to your every whim then die as you see fit."

The Beast barked out another laugh. He flung Cinnia aside so that he could stand and close the rest of the distance to Eoin. Like a shark gliding through murky waters, he moved lightly, effortlessly over uneven ground despite his considerable bulk. When he was within arm's reach, he stopped. His barrel chest expanded while he sampled, as he had before, Eoin's scent.

Cinnia was suddenly beside them, a fidgeting wreck just shy of hysterics. She tugged at the Beast's arm, gentle yet insistent, but he shrugged her off. He swept his tongue over prominent fangs to catch the drool glistening like amber in the firelight.

"If death is what you seek, little knight, surely there are less painful ways to find it."

"But none which I deserve."

Again, the Beast laughed. Tension filled the space between them as he took Eoin's chin in one hand and, with the other, raked his claws across Eoin's scalp. Although the pain was intense, the skin remained intact, proof of how well-versed he was in the limits of mortal flesh, no doubt due to years of experimentation conducted upon his enslaved bride.

Anger bled through Eoin's passive demeanour, but he suppressed it and trembled dramatically. "You see, you haven't simply humbled me. You've destroyed me. The man I used to be is gone. I'm a stranger to my own soul and cannot live this way."

"You tempt me," crooned the Beast, scratching down the length of Eoin's spine to where sweat pooled at the small of his back. "With your pretty words and your pretty, pretty face."

Cinnia began to say something, but the Beast swept out his arm and sent her flying to the right, where she struck rock. Eoin yelped. Every inch of his body demanded he run to her, though he couldn't because the Beast had moved between them so as to better admire the red sparkle of blood leaking from Cinnia's nose.

I've made a terrible mistake.

His heart thumped against his ribcage so fast that Eoin assumed everyone heard it. He couldn't breathe because of the sweltering heat, and panic only added to this. His legs shook. Head filled with fluidic pressure.

I should have known I couldn't do this.

That was quite enough of that.

He reclaimed his wits with a figurative slap. Nothing else mattered save Cinnia. Not his doubts. Not his pride. He had to protect her, had to keep the Beast engaged, regardless of what that meant and how the mere thought of it made his stomach heave. Without giving himself time to change his mind, he pulled the Beast back to him and crashed their mouths together.

"Fight me," he begged after he broke the kiss. "Do whatever else you want to me, but fight me first."

The Beast leered at him. "What a delight you are! Yet you must think me a fool, else you think yourself exceptionally clever."

"I'm sure I don't know what you mean."

"You hope this reluctant seduction will trick me into mercy, is that it?"

"Mercy is for the weak and were you weak, I wouldn't be here asking for what I ask."

"But what you ask is hardly a question. Stay down!" he spat to Cinnia as she braced herself against the rock wall and tried to wobble upright.

Assured of her obedience, he circled Eoin as if in appraisal. Eoin stood frozen, distracting himself with shadows frolicking on the ceiling high above, but when the Beast's finger traced the curve of Eoin's hip down to his thigh, he whined with unease. This spurred the Beast on. He kneaded the hard planes of Eoin's chest as he pressed into Eoin from behind.

"You were always going to die, little knight. From the instant you dared return to me, the life she bought for you was once again mine."

"Just kill him then!" Cinnia cried. "Do it now! Get it over with! Kill him! I can't... You..."

Her pleas devolved into guttural shrieks as she again collapsed upon the ground. Tears sprung to Eoin's eyes. He wanted so much to comfort her, but the Beast held him close and refused to let go. He loved this. Every bit of it.

"You won't force her to watch, will you?" Eoin asked as though he wasn't already certain of the answer.

"She needs reminding of what she is and who I am."

"Then I suppose you'll want this to last as long as possible."

"That would be best, yes."

"Some rules might help."

"I'm listening."

"First, Cinnia has no part in this. You won't hurt her to distract me."

"If you insist," he sighed playfully. "And?"

"As I've already asked, you will fight in this form."

He ground his pleasure against Eoin's backside. "Obviously. And?"

Eoin's voice came out thin and reedy when he said, "I can

defend myself with such weaponry as I see fit."

"Very well. And?"

"You will refrain from the use of fire."

"How dull," the Beast pouted, stepping back.

"But necessary. I've seen the…supremacy of your flames. I've nothing to protect myself from them."

"That's half the fun."

"So you mean to honour Cinnia's request and kill me straightaway?"

At this, Cinnia uncurled from the ball she'd made of herself. Blood had smeared over her cheeks and thickened into gelatinous clumps that stuck to her hair. It was from beneath this sticky mess she peered at them. *Bless you*, Eoin wanted to say, because the Beast, consummate sadist that he was, took one look at her anguish and agreed to Eoin's terms without further debate.

That left just one last detail concerning him.

"You must pardon me, my Lord," Eoin said cautiously, "for I mean no disrespect, but how are we to keep this honest?"

"Don't you trust me?"

"Would you?"

The Beast crossed his arms and chuckled.

"I do trust her, though."

Saying nothing else, Eoin moved towards Cinnia. A little too eagerly perhaps, as the Beast's mouth pulled into a frown, so Eoin tried to keep his expression a blank. Only when his back was to the Beast did he let everything he felt show upon his face. Cinnia stared up in confusion, but then she gasped. She'd seen it. His hope.

She shook her head. She didn't believe in hope. Why would she? After all these years, she must think it a lie, just some simpering snippet of nothing contrived by mothers to pacify their children. Well, if he couldn't convince her with a look, a touch might make the difference. He held out his hand. She grimaced, indicating with a point of her chin that he take heed, that the Beast watched. Eoin didn't care. She needed this, and so did he.

At length, though she looked unsure as to why, she relented. She slipped her hand into Eoin's, and softly, secretly, he caressed the hollow of her palm. She shivered. That pushed things too far. The Beast snarled and Eoin released her, although it physically pained him to do so.

"Is this really what you want?" she asked.

"Yes."

"Blood. He cannot break a blood oath."

Eoin smiled. He pressed his fingers first to his lips then to his heart and pretended not to hear her mewl of distress when he turned to the Beast, who eyed them in dark disapproval. With the crook of an unnervingly long finger, he beckoned Eoin back to him. Eoin obeyed, his legs sturdier than they'd been before. He even dared to kick at some of the treasure he'd previously been careful not to disturb. A jewelled chalice clattered to the edge of the abyss where the heat of the inferno blackened it almost instantly.

"Well? What say you, my Lord?"

The Beast's jaw, which had locked in annoyance, relaxed again. Eoin could almost see the ugly thoughts parading through the Beast's mind, saw himself thoroughly defeated and despoiled, chained up to rot until even the smothering clouds of smoke couldn't keep the flies away. He saw himself driven insane, screeching unintelligibly and desperate for death. Worst of all, he saw Cinnia there for every single second of it.

How many sons would she have to bear before Eoin was allowed to die? He didn't want to know the answer.

He took his bottom lip between his teeth and chomped down for all he was worth. The Beast drew a sharp breath. The blood dribbling down Eoin's chin had him panting. He yanked Eoin into his arms with unprecedented urgency as he bit his own mouth, releasing an inky flow that had the consistency of tar and the putrid stench of weeks old death. This kiss was more of a battle than the last. The Beast moaned, angling his head to better suck what blood escaped his greedy tongue. The more he tasted, the rougher he became. He pawed at Eoin, hands sneaking beneath his clothing, groping every inch of flesh within reach, marking it as his own with bruises. Stars burst in Eoin's eyes. Vomit rushed upwards to defend against the awful, burning mouthfuls he managed to swallow. He could feel it eating through the lining of his throat, could feel his body spasm in violent rejection of what was surely a sin against nature itself, but he had to keep it down. The pact must be made.

When it was finally over and Eoin was free to breathe again, the first thing he choked out was, "Is it done?"

The Beast wore a drunkard's grin. "For all the good it will do you. I'll enjoy this, little knight."

"As will I."

And while the Beast still swooned over Eoin's taste, and before he knew what was happening, Eoin slipped an arrowhead—collected from the carnage outside and hidden in his sleeve—into his fist. He punched it forward, straight towards the Beast's left eye, and praised every god in existence that his aim was true.

The Beast had no reaction at first. In a daze, he plucked the arrowhead from the weeping socket. Could this have been the first he felt of pain? He mustn't have liked it very much, for he screeched pathetically. He tried to strike back but slashed only air as Eoin had already jumped away.

Keeping the Beast in sight, Eoin sprinted about the cavern in search of the sword laid with ivory and emeralds. He'd counted on finding it again, but there was so much treasure, and even half-blinded, the Beast was so fast. Eoin needed more time.

"Now!" he yelled, and for an uncomfortably long moment,

with the ground shaking and the Beast raging, he feared the worst.

If he'd been deceived…

If they didn't come…

But then they soared into the cavern, blasting past Eoin in a writhing whirlwind of vengeance. They slammed into the Beast and he, focused as he was on Eoin, hadn't thought to brace for impact. He was knocked down. His children swarmed over him, using their inheritance to gouge holes through his armour and rip out chunks of flesh. More pain. More of that which he'd ever been so keen to inflict on others. It overwhelmed him. He shrieked and squealed, just like the pig he was.

"Traitors!"

Bewilderment gave way to outrage. He rallied and threw off all six at once, scattering them to every direction, then launched himself at Eoin, who leapt aside in the nick of time. Coins splashed about, slipping against the soles of Eoin's boots so that he couldn't run with any sort of speed. The Beast nearly snatched hold of him. There was a tug on his back. He heard cloth ripping, felt wet heat quicken between his shoulder blades long before he felt the sting of the wound. It could have been worse, but it was awfully close to disastrous.

When the Beast lunged again, Eoin crouched and kicked out his leg in an arc. It caught the Beast soundly behind his knee. He fell, giving Eoin the chance to escape. Better still, in those seconds gained, he found the sword. It was as if it called out to him, as it had done when he'd discovered it outside the lair. His fingers curled around the grip. A strange sense of peace washed over him.

I can do this.

I will do this.

The Beast slowed his advance. His remaining eye was but a glowing slit, and he stared at Eoin as though for the first time. What was he plotting now? Or could it be…?

Was he afraid?

Yes, that was it! He *was* afraid! His children had successfully compromised his scaled armour. There were many openings through which Eoin could sink a blade. He who had presumed immortality now faced the prospect of death, and it terrified him.

"She'll pay for this," the Beast hissed through bared teeth. "You know that, don't you? I'll break every bone in her body! I'll eat her alive, piece by piece!"

Eoin would not be goaded into responding. He charged. The Beast blocked the attack with his forearms, and they strained against one another until he threw Eoin back. Undaunted, Eoin pressed forward, guided by years of muscle memory. This was the reason he'd learned the smell of crushed grass. His duty was not to the tree but to Cinnia alone. This was his final test, and he would not fail.

He focused on the fight, on staying one step ahead and

exploiting what weaknesses he could find. The Beast favoured his right side where his injuries were deepest, so Eoin feigned to the left. When the Beast moved to follow, Eoin seized his chance. The Beast howled. Dark blood sizzled along the sword's edge as Eoin pulled it back.

A good start, though he had best not get too confident. Even wounded, the Beast was still fast, still strong, and angrier than Eoin had yet seen him. It took everything he had to defend against an onslaught of frenzied strikes, but just the fact that he *could* defend himself was enough to unhinge the Beast even further. He stumbled over his plunder. Missed more than one chance to deal Eoin real damage. He cursed and snarled, belly aglow with fire that would have cremated Eoin were it not for the pact they'd made.

A tiny shadow scurried forth to join the fray. Ronan wrapped himself around the Beast's shin and worked his catlike teeth where the flesh was thinnest. Eoin tried to use this distraction to his advantage, but the Beast bounded clear across the cavern.

"Filthy cheater! Did you think I'd let you get away with *this*?!" He tore his son from his ankle and raised him up accusingly. "That there won't be consequences?" And then without any indecision, he ripped Ronan in two.

It took several heartbeats for Eoin to understand what had just happened. It only became real once Cinnia ran past, a blur of red hair, to cradle the mess that was her murdered child.

"No, no, no, no, no," she chanted.

"Is that regret I hear? Is that pain? Your pain is just beginning, slut. I will—"

"No," said Eoin. "You're never going to touch her again."

"I don't have to touch her to hurt her."

With an earth-shattering roar, the Beast shot into the air. Wings burst from his arms, and he swooped about the cavern like a huge, hellish bat.

"Coward! Come down here and face me!"

"Don't fret, little knight, I haven't forgotten you. But for now…"

He went after Liadhnan first, who was closest and couldn't fly properly because of his tattered wings. Eoin pleaded for the others to go to their brother's aid, but before they could, the Beast caught Liadhnan and promptly bit off his head.

"Stop!" Cinnia bawled. "Leave them alone!"

But the Beast was on to the next, barrelling towards Quillan at lightning speed. Eoin tried to call the boy to him, but Quillan was too terrified to listen. He flew stupidly in ever smaller circles until the Beast snapped him up. His blood poured onto Cinnia's head, mixing with that of Ronan and Liadhnan so that she was soaked through. The Beast wheeled around to laugh at her. She screamed back, but it wasn't a scream of fear or even of sorrow. It was anger. With it, she transformed into the witch Eoin had met in the woods, all ice and passion and savage glory.

"Damn you," she said in a low, husky voice.

The Beast was dumbfounded. He'd likely never seen this side of Cinnia, this imperious will with which she faced every other man. Caught in her stare, he didn't notice Áedgen speeding towards him. They collided in cosmic fury, summoning an explosion from the abyss that scorched the ceiling and consumed a good five feet of land.

Wasting no time, Eoin rushed to Cinnia. "Go," he ordered, pushing her to the cavern's entrance just as effulgent fissures began to split the ground.

She opened her mouth to argue, but a shriek cut her off. Áedgen was defeated. The Beast slammed him down and came in for the kill.

"No!" Cinnia shouted, throwing herself on top of her son. "No more!"

"That's right," said the Beast. "No more games. No more mercy. The world will drown in blood. Every last man, woman, and child will die cursing your name, witch!"

Vibrant yellow streaked his throat, and Eoin saw his intention. The Beast had found a loophole in their pact. He'd promised not to hurt Cinnia to distract Eoin, but he hadn't promised not to kill her. With a yell, Eoin leapt in front of her, shielding her as she shielded Áedgen, just as the Beast belched out a lungful of flames.

All that struck them was a wall of pressure, a booming shock wave of failed magic. The Beast had sworn to fight Eoin as a man, not a dragon, and the blood they'd exchanged held him to that. The spell doused his fires. His wings were lost. He plummeted to the earth like a dying star, and Eoin ran to catch him with his sword.

He carved a chunk from the Beast's upper arm, another from his thigh. Wailing, the Beast fought back. He took strips of skin from Eoin's chest and would have taken more if Eoin hadn't danced away.

"You can't save her," the Beast growled. "You can't even save yourself."

"And yet I'm still here."

"Not for long."

A bar of silver smacked against the side of the Beast's head. Cinnia's arms were full with a mix of treasure and rocks, and Eoin cheered as she hurled handfuls of it while shouting an impressive variety of obscenities. This hurt little more than the Beast's pride, yet even that was enough. He took his eye off Eoin for but a second. It was a costly mistake. Lunging forward, Eoin stabbed through the Beast's gut. He hiccupped, face softening into a likeness of questioning innocence, as Eoin twisted the sword before pulling it out. Black, hissing blood coated the length of the blade. The Beast whimpered, and that whimper grew into a groan.

Then the world broke apart.

The abyss erupted once more into a hellscape. Boulders smashed down all around, spraying lava and liquid gold. Splits in the cavern's floor that had previously been nuisances widened to looming chasms into which the ocean of riches began to drain. Eoin was caught in the surging tide, borne along waves of silver and gold, deafened by the clatter.

His fingers snagged the barest edge of rock. He tried to pull himself up, but treasure beat relentlessly against his back, and his arms were losing what strength they had. It couldn't end like this. Not when he was so close to achieving his goal.

He shouted out, "Please!" and then small hands wrapped around his wrist. Cinnia dug her heels into the crumbling earth and tugged hard enough to practically pop his shoulder from its socket. Yelling, forcing himself through the pain, he found purchase with his feet, helping her as she yanked him back up.

She was gone before he was able to stand. It was a mystery how she kept her balance as the shaking hadn't stopped, only gotten worse, but she was quick and spry. Eoin saw she'd made it back across to the other side of the cavern where the Beast wept in a twitching heap. Those same little hands that had saved Eoin now grabbed up the sword that still lay where he had dropped it. By the time he reached her, she'd begun to scream out what sounded like nonsense, though was, in fact, a list.

"No more rape! No more deals! No more curses! No more death!"

With each declaration, she drove the sword down in the Beast, ripped it out, and plunged it in again. As his mouth gaped in what Eoin could only describe as disbelief, the Beast tried to lift a shuddering hand towards Cinnia as though he actually expected her to take it and comfort him as he died. She cackled with glee then spat on his face, continuing to hack away at him until the blade, weakened by the caustic blood spouting up like a fountain, shattered. Cinnia's red, watering eyes were wild with ruthless ecstasy. Her laugh was like nothing Eoin had ever heard before. She was terrifying really, bathed as she was in blood, a vampiric fairy feasting after a thousand-year fast. And she wasn't done yet. She flung the remains of the sword aside to reach for the largest rock she could lift. Straddling the Beast, the monster who had terrorised and tortured her for years, Cinnia cracked open his head and smashed what was within until nothing remained save pulp.

"No more," she finished breathlessly.

Trembling in awe, Eoin called her name. She gave half a smile then tumbled away from the Beast and into Eoin's waiting arms. They lay panting—hands in each other's hair, on each other's faces, legs tangled together—until the earth stopped shaking and the fires fizzled out.

Squinting through the sudden darkness, Cinnia and Eoin looked to one another for reassurance, found none, and so looked back at the Beast's corpse, fully expecting him to rise again with meteoric vengeance, but minutes crawled by and this did not happen. Nothing happened. The nightmare was over. Warmth spread from somewhere low in Eoin's chest. His soul sang, his heart was a merry drum. And the pain... He was slick with gore and sweat, his injuries too numerous to count, yet he was so drunk with bliss that he hardly noticed the pain. It had been so long since he'd felt this good, too long, and he scarcely knew what to do with himself. He hid his face in the crook of Cinnia's neck while mute laughter tickled his throat.

"You've done it!" he cried, choking on a flood of happiness. "You've killed him!"

Several moments passed before she moved and, even then, it was only to blink. He helped her to a sitting position.

"Cinnia, you're free!"

"Free?" she squeaked.

"Praise the gods, yes! The Beast is dead!"

Her hand was a vice on his arm. Her eyes bore into his. She went from holding her breath to turning it loose in short, successive gasps as her mind worked at speeds too swift for the rest of her body to follow. Eoin watched her conquer doubt, saw how her drooping mouth formed into a perfect 'O' as euphoria unfurled across her face. Suddenly, they were laughing together. They couldn't stop if they tried; the release was far too sweet. Eoin threw his arms around her, almost toppling them over again. She clung to him so that it seemed they'd never come apart. Her tears were hot against his cheek, so different from the heat of the flames, so clean and pure. He wept as well. Like the laughter, it was impossible to suppress.

His thoughts then became a prismatic jumble. Cinnia in the

sunshine. Flowers in her hair. Her hand warm in his as they searched through tide pools and waded into the sleepy blue sea. All the beauty she'd been denied, he would give to her. He would dedicate his life to the fulfilment of every dream she ever had. Cinnia grabbed his face in her hands, holding him steady as if to peer into the future he planned for them. She'd a boldness about her he hadn't seen before, unexpected though certainly not unwelcome. He didn't dare move. When her gaze drifted to his lips, he gulped, hoping the blush scalding his cheeks wasn't as conspicuous as it felt.

A ghastly screech wrenched them apart.

Oisín.

Blood spurted from the little one's gaping mouth, drowning his screams in sickening gurgles, yet he still dragged himself towards them, reaching out for help. And there, squatting on his back, was Áedgen. He smirked, proudly showing off the ragged ribbons of flesh stuck between his teeth. With one more duck of his head, Oisín's screams came to an abrupt end.

A moment of silence passed. Then Cinnia wailed so that Eoin's heart splintered, but all his attention remained upon Áedgen as the boy made a show of pointing to a spot just behind Eoin's shoulder. He wasn't sure what it was Áedgen wanted him to see. There were only slabs of rock and mounds of blackened treasure. But there it was! A flash of movement. A small head. Tiny eyes whose pupils were blown wide with terror.

Cáelán.

Eoin darted forward. His legs were so weak they gave out, but he was up again in the next breath, racing to throw himself between the two brothers.

He did not make it.

Áedgen took to wing, hurtling past Eoin, bursting through piles of jingling coins. Cáelán was snatched into the air. There was a flash of claws. An arching spray of blood. Áedgen cackled triumphantly and dropped Cáelán's mangled body at Eoin's feet.

Cinnia was still wailing, hadn't stopped since she'd first begun. "Why?" she asked in a drawn-out whine, a tragic petition to redeem the only child she had left.

Now balanced atop a boulder, Áedgen leisurely licked the red from first one paw then the other. He didn't answer her. Didn't need to. Eoin saw in him the same joy he'd seen the night of the ambush. The same hunger. The *want*. And somehow, Eoin knew what was about to happen. He felt it down to his bones.

As the change took hold, Áedgen threw back his head with vicious laughter. He didn't have to alter his size as the Beast had done, only his shape. His neck straightened. Taut ropes of muscles snaked around his wings, fashioning them into human arms. His tail vanished up his spine, adding bulk to his back and shoulders. He stood tall on two strong legs, a demon prince dressed in scales and crowned in flaming red hair.

Áedgen stared down at himself in wonder, raising his hands, flexing his fingers, but this didn't last long. Cinnia swivelled at the hips as if making ready to run, but even without wings, Áedgen still flew with the speed of shadows to block her escape.

"Beautiful," he croaked, running a forked tongue along his lipless mouth. "Mine."

CHAPTER 13

The fires that withered when the Beast took his last breath burst back into life, demolishing what remained of the stalactites above. A hail of rock rained down upon Eoin's head. Although he tried to shield himself, one sizeable chunk bounced off his temple. His sight went black and nothingness echoed in his ears. Cinnia was the guide who ushered him through the darkness. She was crying, bleating like a lamb flung into a wolf's den. Eoin crawled towards her until his vision returned, but the sight that greeted him nearly sent him reeling back into oblivion.

Áedgen, truly his father's son, had Cinnia trapped in a steely grip. Though she pled for him to stop and frantically tried to wriggle free, her efforts only served to excite him. He leered at her panic. He licked her skin and purred lecherously.

Disgust blistered Eoin's throat like another draught of the Beast's poisoned blood. After having anger as his constant companion these last weeks, he thought he'd learned of its depths, but all that had come before was merely preparation for what he now experienced. His cry was as a thunderclap splitting the heavens asunder. Áedgen barely glanced up from Cinnia's neck before Eoin rammed into him with the might of a horned god. He was the king of holly and of oak, lord of both death and resurrection. His fists flew fast, hard, and forced Áedgen backwards until he hit the cave wall.

"You will not have her!" Eoin bellowed, punctuating each word with another brutal strike. "I won't let you!"

His knuckles broke. His wrists were in danger of the same. A normal opponent would be dead, yet Áedgen was far from normal, and although the anger coursing through Eoin was restorative, it wouldn't perform miracles. His pace was already beginning to slow. To win, he must be clever. He must be quick.

He stepped back. Áedgen was panting, but a broad grin stretched across his hateful face. Good. Let the vile prince think the battle was his to lose. Eoin looked at Cinnia, at the pitiful slump of her shoulders, the corpse-like pallor of her skin. All the icy strength she'd summoned to kill the Beast was gone, and she was drained and defeated. He needed her to see that he was not.

"Cinnia," he called, catching her eyes, willing her to hold on to hope.

"Mine," Áedgen insisted.

Eoin ignored him. "Neither men nor women are trees, Cinnia. The only duty you have is to your own heart, your own happiness. You are free."

Then he laughed until Áedgen screeched and threw himself about like a child in a temper over a toy. His chest glowed orange then yellow as Eoin took stock of his position, of his surroundings, and when a thin stream of fire spat from Áedgen's mouth, Eoin dove aside, landing precisely where he wanted.

Áedgen roared in frustration. To mock him, Eoin roared too. He stood, beckoning Áedgen closer with one hand while hiding the other behind his back. The boy was too blinded by wounded pride to see what Eoin held, what he had plucked from the rubble. He knew nothing of patience nor of sacrifice, and so it didn't surprise Eoin when he, in an explosion of demonic flesh, reverted to his true form.

But Eoin was ready for this. He didn't try to run. Áedgen leapt at him. Eoin raised his free arm to guard his throat against biting teeth and brought the other, the one he'd kept hidden, forward. When Áedgen struck him, they toppled backwards so that Áedgen fell upon both Eoin and the jagged shards of the sword that had killed the Beast. What was left of the blade slipped into the largest of the three slashes his brothers had cut across his chest. Eoin lifted the boy just enough to wrench the blade out then drive it in even deeper. Áedgen's weight took on a new heft. Hot blood gushed out over Eoin's fingers, and only once the torrent slowed to a gentle rain did he cast the sword aside.

Sitting up, he slid Áedgen into his lap. The eyes inherited from Cinnia showed only fear. The hunger was gone. So was the insanity. Because of this, he looked more human than ever before, a frightened child staring out from behind the mask of a monster.

"Mother," he groaned.

She came to him at once. "My son, I forgive you," she murmured, pressing kisses onto his cooling skin. "Please, *please*, forgive me."

The flames of the inferno were but dying embers. With no heir left to claim the Beast's throne, they would not rise again. An influx of air wafted in from the cavern's entrance, clean and light, a gift for overworked lungs. Eoin was dizzy, his head a drifting cloud, yet he still had enough presence of mind to feel the exact moment Áedgen's bedevilled soul soared off into the ether. Cinnia felt it too, and her whispered apologies shattered like glass.

She didn't speak for weeks, wouldn't so much as shrug or nod when asked a question. Mostly she slept, and Eoin told himself this was a good thing. When they were strong enough, he spirited her away from her wooded prison with what food remained and what gold he could carry.

"So you never find yourself in want of anything. So you

can live in the comfort you deserve," he told her, half expecting her to protest against taking the ill-gotten riches for herself. He needn't have bothered. She only stared through him to some invisible place he'd begun to resent.

At least she was willing to follow where he led. He took to calling her his little duckling, as she was always two steps behind him. If he stopped short, she would bump into his back and wait there until he moved forward again. For a while, he tried to make this a game but couldn't coax her into laughter or even the smallest of smiles.

He missed both. He needed both. But he would not risk upsetting her by telling her so.

The Accursed Lands were cursed no more, and thus a change had begun in them. The winds were fresh and the skies shone blue. As Eoin and Cinnia journeyed further and further away from the forest, he pointed out those pretty things that were able to flourish now that the boil poisoning them had been lanced. Though she looked at them obediently, he couldn't tell whether she gained pleasure from them. Yet he pressed on. Here, starlight glittering in a singing brook. There, a budding field of golden grain. He found roses blooming in subtle shades of pink between the cracks of a forgotten stone fence and was about to pick one for her before deciding against it. Instead, he bent down to smell them, inviting Cinnia to do the same. She didn't even seem to see them, but when she caught their scent, she shivered as if splashed by water. Soon she was stroking a thoughtful finger across soft petals, and Eoin's heart felt fit to burst.

Later that day, she said, "Thank you," when he lifted her over a patch of mud along the road. Then that evening, she bid him, "Goodnight," when he tucked her into her bedroll. After both instances, he allowed himself a breath's worth of hope, which led to another and then another and another. By the time he laid down his head, it was crowded with indulgent dreams that had spun quite beyond his control.

Honestly, he ought to have known better.

His rude awakening came well past midnight when he discovered her kneeling before the campfire, flinging her hand above the flames with the abandon of a zealot.

"What are you doing?" he asked, rubbing sleep from his eyes.

At his voice, she sped up her movements, and light bounced off the edge of the dagger she held.

"Cinnia, don't!"

"Leave me be," she snarled, as she sawed through another hank of her glorious red hair. "I hate it! I can't stand to look at it! I want it gone, all of it!"

She'd barely thrown the hair into the fire before she tore out the next handful by the roots. Angry gashes glistened here and there on her now half-bald head. Eoin's pulse leapt. His fingers twitched. But he left her to her work. She had to do this for herself. There were some evils he couldn't protect her from, wounds that only she could heal.

"I'd cut it all away if I could. My loathsome face. My breasts. My sex. All of it!" A shudder rolled down her body. She followed its path, doubling over, mumbling so that he could only hear bits of what she said. "…disgusting, so dirty…don't want it, I don't want it, I don't want it!"

She let loose a gut-wrenching scream, and blood spurted from the largest gouge yet. Horrified, he snatched the dagger from her clammy grip, and immediately, all her raving wrath turned to him. Spitting out a string of curses, she beat against his chest with fists clenched, then sobbed and apologised, only to curse again. Eoin shushed her as though she were a sickly child, and when she finally went still, he continued the task she had started.

"We'll keep your hair as short as you'd like. We can bind your breasts and dress you as a man if that will make you happy. Or cover you with great, billowing robes if that will bring you peace. Anything, Cinnia. If you wish it, it shall be done. Your body is your own."

With that, he cut away the last lock of hair. While she slowly, almost reverently, ran her fingers over her scalp, acquainting herself with the feel of it, he only pretended to burn what hair he held in his hand. On the urging of his heart, he instead stuffed it into his boot.

She glanced sideways at him. He thought he'd been caught out, but she asked, "Why are you so good to me?"

He softly chuckled, brushing his knuckles against her cheek, and she leaned into him but then, flinching, jerked away.

"You wouldn't be so kind if you knew."

"Knew what, Cinnia?"

"That I'm glad," she said in a sibilant whisper. "I'm glad," she said again, louder, as if it was a question, her mouth somewhere between a smile and a scream. "My babies are dead, and I am glad for it! I'm a monster! I'm the witch they always claimed I was!"

Words failed him. He threw his arms around her and hoped that would suffice, but she wailed like someone very close to death.

"I'm glad too!" he blurted out, admitting his innermost shame. "I'm as much a witch as you."

"I was their *mother*."

"You still are. You love them despite everything done to you, even though anyone would understand if you couldn't." He took her face into his hands. "And they knew this. They were willing to die for you because of it."

She met his conviction with a grim smirk. "I should have been the one to die."

"That's not true. They wanted you to live, Cinnia."

"But what if I don't?" Her stare darkened, and she gestured to the dagger that lay beside them. "Eoin, if I...? Should I want to die, will you let me?"

He shut his eyes in an effort to weaken looming despair, to

cling to the lie that all she needed was flowers and sunshine and time. A fruitless attempt. She was fading from him. She was going to leave him, and he was terrified and so very tired of pretending he wasn't. His composure was like a fortress made of sand; it washed away as he pulled her against him. Something like a moan caught in his throat. He kissed her temple. He kissed her cheek. His lips slid over her skin, tasting the salt of her tears. She was so pliant in his arms, so perfect, and he wanted to say that he... Gods, but he wanted. And she knew. How could she not?

"Only if I can die with you," he breathed into her ear, holding her tighter and tighter still, frantic to keep her, though she was already lost.

CHAPTER 14

hen at long last Eoin stood before the castle gates, he was unrecognisable to even the oldest and dearest of his friends. He was too thin, his beard too woolly, his eyes too wild. Even the way he moved had changed, and he carried himself with such singular purpose that he was granted an immediate audience with the Queen, though the hour was late and there were those still sceptical of his identity.

It was Muireann who laid all doubts to rest. She knew him at once, greeting him with a gasp that ripened to a shout of joy. Eoin had wondered how his heart would behave at their reunion, but now, face to face with her again after so much had passed, he found his response rather sedate. He was not indifferent by any means. He was glad she looked to be well and readily returned her smile, yet he couldn't help but think there ought to be something more, some stirring of the soul or at the least a flustered thrill.

Muireann, for her part, was delighted. Her nose reddened enough to suggest that she might just cry, and after a few moments fighting to keep calm, she eschewed etiquette. Her slippered feet padded across the oaken floor, and, once near, she wrapped her arms around his neck with none of the restraint expected of royalty. Astonished, his own arms hung limp at his sides until he recovered enough sense to catch her elbow in an affectionate albeit clumsy squeeze.

She leaned back, eyes sparkling, but he stopped whatever she meant to say by drawing the remnants of a mighty sword. It was pitted with black, evil blood. Its decorations of emerald and ivory were chipped and scorched. Kneeling, he offered this tainted relic up to her as proof of what all had assumed impossible.

"The Beast is dead."

Weeks went by in a blur. The days grew shorter, the nights colder, and life took the shape that Eoin believed it would remain in forevermore. At first, he had grudgingly attended a ridiculous amount of meetings and assemblies, feasts and celebrations, where he disappointed throngs of yammering admirers by refusing to relay more than the succinct, heavily censored version of events that he'd told to Muireann, but his tolerance for such banal pageantry wore thin very quickly. He tore up all further invitations and took his meals alone in his room. No one seemed able to understand why. Some rivals of old even tried to circulate rumours that he'd lied, that the Beast yet lived, and that a guilty conscience and the fear of discovery were the reasons for Eoin's self-imposed seclusion. He didn't care a whit. Spite felt more authentic, more trustworthy than fawning flattery did to him of late.

As peace was impossible to find within the castle walls, he began to spend most of his time on horseback, thundering across frozen fields or through silvery woodlands. He was a ghost on the horizon, a dark rider with hair and cloak blowing out behind him like a storm cloud. And if not riding, he was climbing the castle's highest tower so that he could stare out over the ocean, losing himself in the endless dance of waves.

I've always dreamt of the sea.

His father raged. "How dare you shame me like this?!"

His mother despaired. "You've a duty to uphold."

He didn't bother to reply. Silence was fitting revenge against those who had once demanded it, and apart from these occasional barbs, neither parent tried to apply further pressure to him. There was a stain in the depths of his eyes, a distortion in the set of his shoulders that unnerved them, as it did to all who saw what he had become.

Eventually, confirmation of the Beast's demise arrived from the east. Although Eoin's reputation was restored, gentry and peasant alike had by then agreed that he'd lost his mind, and after he beat a man to within an inch of his life for uttering but one harsh word to a little scullery maid, no one wanted to brave his company save Muireann.

She joined him now and then, up in the tower, trying to see what it was that he saw in the water. He argued it was better she didn't see, didn't understand. Some burdens weren't meant to be shared. The set of her jaw told him that she had already discovered this for herself, likely on the day her father the King had died and again when Eoin had gone away.

She'd grown since then. Hardened. The number of counsellors she surrounded herself with had decreased. Those remaining were far more deferential than ever before. Eoin told her that he was proud of her, and he meant it, even if it saddened him to think back on the lively slip of a girl he once shadowed through gardens and corridors.

Apparently following a path of thought similar to his own, she asked, "We both of us have paid a high price, haven't we?"

"Aye," he answered, looking down at her. Not so long ago, he'd have done anything to stand this close to her, to smell the spices in her hair and the oils with which she bathed, to hear each rustling movement of her velvet dress and imagine the peach-like softness of the flesh hidden within it. But now all he wanted was to be left alone.

"Is it worth it, do you suppose?" she went on. "Strength at the cost of our innocence?"

"By that, do you mean to ask whether I would do it all again? Yes, I would. A thousand times over, across a hundred different lives."

Muireann hummed pensively as she leaned against the balustrade. He heard questions in her voice that were as yet unformed, and he had no desire to answer any of them. Remarking upon the weather, he offered her a chance to go inside, back to the warmth of the hearth and friendlier faces.

"I am afraid for you," she said, her smile tight.

"You needn't be."

"Then give me a reason."

Clearly, she wouldn't leave until her curiosity was sated. Silently damning her newfound confidence, he focused on the sea. It was a slumbering giant that day, with opaline skin glittering beneath the dove-grey skies of winter. A fine dusting of snow melted against Eoin's brow. He let out a heavy breath, which crystallised in the frosty air.

"What would you have me say? A trite reference to time? Some vague assurances I cannot promise to keep? I am here. I am alive. Is that not enough?"

Patience exhausted, he started to walk away from her. She stopped him by catching his hand and stroked the braid of red hair tied around his wrist.

"I'm told your sleep is troubled," she said, almost cruel in her candour. "That your dreams are violent, unrelenting. Your page says you often cry out a woman's name."

Eoin's mouth, which hung open, snapped shut. "He has no business concerning you with such things, my Queen."

"No. Whilst we two are alone, hidden from the circling

buzzards of court, let us do away with titles and the nonsense that comes with them." She spoke plainly but could not conceal from him her annoyance. She wanted something from Eoin. They all did. But while the others were now too afraid to ask, she was not. Gathering as much height as she could into her diminutive frame, she declared, "Let us be Muireann and Eoin, as we once were."

"As you wish," he replied woodenly.

"But what do *you* wish?"

"Does it matter?"

"That is unfair." Her sprinkling of light, brown freckles sunk into a hectic flush that had nothing to do with the cold. "Why are you so angry? Why must you push away everyone who cares for you?"

There was a strain upon his chest, a simmering mix of resentment and pain that was as familiar as the nearly constant ache in his shoulder, but Muireann bore no fault for that. He softened his stance. Placing his hand atop hers in apology, he took a moment to compose an answer kind enough to honour their years of friendship.

"I have seen into the heart of evil," he said at length. "I see it still. It has changed me, altered the very essence of who I am."

"Yet you say you would do it all again."

"Yes."

She brushed the bracelet of hair with her thumb. "Because

of her?"

"Yes."

"Who is she?"

"A dream," he whispered, though his throat fought against him. "A ghost."

"Then… She's dead?"

But he was distracted, searching the sky for a shade of blue that matched the eyes he yearned to see. And because he could not find it there, he looked inward, shuffling through memories as though they were sheets of parchment stored in a chest of drawers. There it was. Sapphire streaked with silver. Secretive. Consuming. Divine.

Those oceanic eyes drew him in, and he was helpless with dread, fingers grasping for something to which he could keep hold.

"Cinnia, what have you done?"

"Shhh, all is well. Lie back. Let me sing you to sleep."

A strange bitterness coated his tongue and warned him of the potion she'd slipped into his drink. He tried to spit it up, but it was too late. He sank into its effects as into bathwater, mind and body both impossibly sluggish. Drawing his head upon her lap, she carded her fingers through his hair, petting him as if he was a kitten, although she was the one who purred.

"I'm beg…begging… Cinnia… Please."

She fluttered out of focus. Her wordless lullaby filled his ears, beautiful and sad and seeming to stretch across a great distance. Tears splashed down onto his face, mingling with his own, but neither they nor the kiss she tenderly placed on his lips was enough to break the spell. When he awoke, she was gone, and all he had left was a token of hair to convince him that he hadn't merely imagined her.

"Eoin?" Muireann called, rousing him from this, the last of his memories of Cinnia. "Is she dead?"

He shook his head, adamantly rejecting what the most perverse parts of him feared to be true. That poison could not be allowed to spread. He must have faith that Cinnia would endure, regardless of the trials she may face. This was, after all, the reason the Beast had chosen her. It was not her beauty he wanted but her strength. She was as a supple green reed, able to grow in whichever direction she was bent. She was a force of nature with an adaptive, indomitable will. She wasn't dead. She was somewhere out there, learning what it meant to be free. Happy, Eoin hoped, or on the way to happiness. Living for his sake until she could live for her own.

Sunlight spiked through the clouds, and though it was such a pale yellow so as to be nearly white, its rays cut a jewelled path across the sea. Was that a sign?

Muireann was speaking. It took a great deal of effort to force his concentration back to her.

"I prithee you will excuse me, my Queen, but I haven't heard a thing you've said."

"Muireann," she corrected. "I asked where she is."

"I don't know."

"And if you did, would you still have come back home?"

"No."

Tiny creases gathered across her forehead. "Well, well. I'm relieved to find that you're not quite as different as you allege to be. I always could trust you to supply a healthy measure of blunt honesty."

"I meant no offence."

She gave a cavalier laugh. The wind frolicked through her golden hair and loosened strands from an intricate arrangement of ribbons, plaits, and pearls. She batted them from her eyes, looking so fiercely spirited that Eoin smiled at her in genuine affection. Taking up her hand, he pressed it between his own.

"My Queen. Muireann. I feel I should tell you that there was a time when—"

"I know. I've always known. And had circumstances been different, I—"

"But they weren't. And here we are."

"Here we are," she agreed with one slow, grave nod.

He released her hand. They stood in silence side by side, equals at last, comfortable in the awareness that their bond, although tied together with new knots, had not been broken. Eoin relaxed into the moment, and his gaze once again roved across the water.

So trapped was he in the rhythmic pull of the tides that he didn't discern how closely Muireann watched him. He was more handsome than ever, she mused. His adventures had stripped his face of its youthful charms, revealing chiselled lines of maturity that were as refined and dignified as they were alluring. But he was still far too young to have eyes that old. Like twin parasites, longing and anger fed on him and would bleed him dry should they remain unchecked. That mustn't happen. She would not abide it.

She hemmed to regain his attention. "I thought of naming you my champion."

A small sigh. "I'm honoured."

"I said 'I thought.' Not 'I will.'"

He bowed his head, conceding his mistake. An elfin humour took hold of her suddenly. It played with the curve of her blush pink lips.

"Shall I tell you a secret, Eoin?"

This sigh was more substantial than the last. "If you'd like."

She giggled. He'd tired of her company but was too polite to admit it. Ever the gentleman and so easy to tease. She wove her arm through his.

"Pride is a rigid, fragile thing," she said as if lecturing a child. "Thus, great lengths are taken to protect it."

He feigned interest with a low noise from his throat.

"I have learned, over the years, how to spot someone preoccupied with the defence of their pride. Some will bluster. Some will lie. Some lash out, finding threats where there are none. All because pride, to them, eclipses everything else."

She paused. She could tell he listened, much as he'd prefer otherwise.

"Then there are those for whom the opposite is true. It isn't pride they serve but humility. They will defer before they argue, give before they take. Sacrifice comes second nature to them, and they are happiest when they are of use to others. How different life could be if the rest of us followed the example they set, but, sadly, in this world ruled by pride, where humility is so often dismissed as weakness, they're beaten down and taught they are unworthy. I wish it weren't so. I wish they could see what I see."

She reached up two fingers, using them to direct his face towards hers. She wanted there to be no confusion or room for debate.

"I see—I've always seen—a beautiful soul and a boundless heart. Not perfect, no, but noble and good and strong. So very strong. You are enough, Eoin, just as you are. Why then do you deny yourself? Go to her."

His brow shot up in surprise. Gooseflesh broke out over his skin. Muireann smiled.

"*Go.*"

"She…" His voice cracked. "She does not want me."

"Is that true, or is it simply what you fear?"

"Well, she… I…"

"Shall I tell you another secret? Like attracts like. We seek ourselves in others, hoping for affirmation of our ideals. So tell me, old friend, about the woman haunting your dreams. Is she burdened, just as you are, by the scars of war? Did the heart of evil change her as it changed you? And if so, isn't it possible that she feels as undeserving of you as you do of her?"

Had he never considered this before? Evidently not. It was truly gratifying to watch him work through his thoughts, probing for those memories that would refute her claim yet uncovering only confirmation instead. The shadows lifted from his face. The dejected line of his shoulders straightened. He was in that instant as eager and full of hope as the day he'd volunteered to fight the Beast. Still, he seemed to need a bit more reassurance.

"I wouldn't know where to look for her."

"I think you do," she replied with a grin.

Eoin's eyes flicked towards the sea and found in it the answers he'd been searching for all this time. Muireann found hers in the bittersweetness of their goodbyes.

There were no flowers or fanfare to see him off on this journey. Only Muireann watched as he rode away into the distance. She had a bit of a cry, although as she'd already mourned this loss once, it wasn't quite so terrible as before. She descended from the tower, not a changed woman but a contented one. Her crown no longer felt a prison nor her future so set in stone, and for this alone, she happily decided that something good could come of love after all.

EPILOGUE

Once upon a time, on the morning after a moonless night, a witch swept like a storm into a sleepy village by the sea. Her head was hooded, her back hunched. Greasy robes dragged behind her in raggedy shreds. She reeked of sheep's dung and wood smoke and the blackest of magics, and she never spoke, not a single word.

When she first skulked into sight, children ran shrieking to hide behind the hedgerows. Women spat over their shoulders as their husbands postured with spears in hand. Yet the witch was undeterred. She pointed to some strings of fleshy, white fish hung up to dry and, grunting, held out a heaping palmful of gold coins.

Now whenever she came to town, the children still ran shrieking but ran towards her instead of away. It had become a game of courage, a boisterous lark that the witch seemed as keen as the children to play. She indulged them with growls and false lunges, and when their screams reached a particularly fevered pitch, she was known to break into rasping cackles.

"Grandmother," the women would then call, beckoning her over. After checking for privacy with a side to side glance, they leaned in to whisper of their troubles. The witch would listen to all such complaints, groaning in sympathy, and then root through her rags for bottled potions or sachets of pungent herbs. So desirous were the women for these remedies, they condescended to let her clasp their arms and pat their cheeks, although this made their skin crawl as if set upon by biting ants.

Next, the merchants would puff out their chests to boom, "Good morning to you, Grandmother." They competed with one another, not with their wares but the warmth of their greetings, for they'd discovered that if met with kindly, honest smiles, she was likely to pay more than she ought.

By and large, it was a satisfactory arrangement for everyone concerned, and as long as she continued to provide money, medicine, and entertainment, she was permitted to live in peace. But it wouldn't take much for that to change. Though generous, though diminished with age, she was a witch, and there were limits to the villagers' begrudging goodwill. In the event of a premature death or an unnatural birth, they'd gladly band together to kill her in the most terrible manner they could stomach.

They don't need to tell her this. The witch instinctively

understands, knows that she walks along a knife's edge. She has escaped misfortune 'til now by stepping as lightly as she can. It's best to live as the wind, to come and go without warning, to keep to the wastes and follow the sun. She avoids well-beaten roads in favour of peatlands and rolling green hills cut with slabs of limestone, and she never—*never*—presumes to think of these people as friends. A witch will not be trusted, and so in turn, a witch doesn't trust.

Only once she is alone, with all trace of civilisation behind her, does she feel safe enough to remove her disguise and drop the act. She straightens her spine. Her stride lengthens. She tips back her head, letting the hood that defends her against hostile eyes fall away. Like a butterfly emerging from its chrysalis, the ancient crone vanishes and a woman of impossible beauty steps forth.

In the final days of winter, when she was half-starved, half-frozen, and more than a little mad, she sought shelter in the ruins of an abandoned hut. Back then, the roof was buckling and the mud plaster was crumbling away from the wickerwork walls, yet she knew she was where she belonged.

She began repairs immediately. Really, it would have been more sensible to start fresh than to pull the hut apart and put it all together again because by the time the work was finished, her hands were nought but raw, weeping clubs. Even this many months later, her knuckles are still swollen. They throb as she shrugs a basket of food from her shoulders and peels off her stinking robes, but she has no regrets. Her hands were a small sacrifice to prove to herself that nothing damaged was without hope of recovery.

She smiles. She never tires of admiring the humble little home she has created. It is snug and tidy. And *hers*. The strands of cockleshells she's collected clatter gaily in the breeze as if welcoming her back. Her garden bursts with colour, and she can't resist pottering about the rows, idling in the heady smell of sun-kissed woodbine.

Soon, the exertion of the long walk to and from the village catches up with her. She's tempted to lie down amongst the sedges and while away the afternoon in dreams, but dreams are dangerous things. They are wont to show her one of three faces, and each comes with their own unique brand of pain.

The first is evil incarnate. It is a sharp grin shining in the dark and claws pinning her down. Molten gold puddles beneath her, swallowing her inch by inch, no matter how she fights. And his laughter... Her dreams recreate it with such tortuous precision that she vomits herself awake.

The second is not one face but many. They scream and they scream and they scream. She digs them out of defiled graves, finds worms and accusations in their eyes, loses one as soon as she reaches for another. They bite at her breasts, and she bleeds guilt for days afterwards.

The last face is handsome and kind. She adores this face.

She sobs from the sheer delight it brings her. But once she wakes, oh, then does she grieve so that she thinks she might die.

To avoid these faces, to protect herself from the misery they inflict, she's learned to sleep as little as possible. It's time to get her blood pumping. She scampers from her garden to the bluffs of black rock just beyond her yard and follows a footpath there down to where the sea timidly brushes against the pebbled shore.

Barely stopping to untie her belt and tear off her dress, she tumbles like a sleek young seal into the waves. They are shockingly cold and steal her breath away, but she doesn't care. She's made weightless. She's made whole. She is one with mysteries older than those found in even the holiest of groves. The water is a goddess, a mother in whose eternal womb she can reshape herself, in whose grace she is reborn into the woman that she could have been—should have been—were it not for the fire.

It truly is a miraculous gift she hadn't expected to receive, yet her greedy, witch's heart dares to want more. She can't resist it, can't refuse it, and so she whispers a wish into the water for that which belongs to another. She wishes she had hair the colour of honey and a castle made of white stone, although it isn't the life of a queen she desires but the love of a man who by now must be king.

Stop it, she scolds herself, blowing a sulking breath into bubbles. She has no right to ask for him, just as she hadn't the right to keep him when she had the chance. She's fully aware that she could have exploited his sense of duty, manipulated him into staying by her side forever. She had *almost* done it. It would have felt so good to surrender to selfishness. But instead, she set him free. She passed her final test.

Maybe this is why her Mother Goddess deigned to grant her the happiness she now enjoys. And at least she has her imagination. Whenever a grey cloud of loneliness looms overhead, she can remember all the conversations she and her gentle king never had and the secrets they never shared. This will suffice to soothe the cries of her rebellious heart.

Or so she'll pretend.

She heads for shore. Above her, pinks and oranges have smudged the sky. The cooling air nips at her as she hurries back into her clothes. She combs a hand through her short, red curls and picks a slow path up the bluffs, occupying her mind with thoughts of supper.

When she crests the summit, she faces the sea to give thanks for the day, but just then, a horse whinnies. Bile floods her throat. She throws herself flat against the earth as a masculine murmur confirms her worst fear, knowing all too well what will happen should a man catch sight of her. Without robes to shroud her comely shape, without a hood to hide her beauty, he will undoubtedly want what a long line of men before him have wanted.

Clawing at handfuls of heather, she draws out one breath after another until the urge to scream recedes. She lifts her head. There's a horse, a spotted roan stallion kicking at the dirt in front of her hut. Just the one horse. One rider then. Two at most. He or they must have gone inside. She considers running back down to the beach but would be trapped there should she be followed. She could make for the moors, but there isn't any cover for miles around. He's going to find her. He's going to…

No.

No!

Her freedom was too hard-won to risk losing again, not after everything she's given up, had taken, lived without, and lived with. Summoning years of repressed rage, her fingers reach for the dagger sheathed on her belt. If she acts fast, she might have the advantage. And supposing there are indeed two of them, well, she'll fight them to her last drop of blood.

She rises to a crouch. The stallion's ears prick, and it nickers a greeting, the stupid thing, betraying her presence. There's no hope for stealth now. She sprints forward, weapon in hand, murder in her eyes. Yet the instant the man ducks out of her doorway, she falls to her knees. The dagger drops from her grasp. And she stares. She just stares. At his dark hair and his pale eyes. At the smile that blooms on his lips when he sees her. When he calls, "Cinnia," in his deep, melodic voice, she bursts into tears.

She's sure she must have somehow sunk into a dream, that

he'll disappear if she opens her eyes, but then she feels his touch upon her arms. She gasps, in thrall to a boneless swoon. He helps her to her feet. Plucking her hands from her face one by one, he repeats her name as softly as a dove cooing in the twilight.

"Cinnia."

"Eoin," she breathes back, meeting his gaze again.

Oh, but he's been crying too! She wipes his cheek dry with her thumb, and he blushes. They are both trembling terribly. He's afraid, she realises, yet hopeful, while she burns with a blend of shame and elation. She has a thousand questions to ask him but can only manage two.

"How...? Why...?"

That lovely blush darkens. He bows his head, embarrassed perhaps or overwhelmed. His hair hides his face, and this simply will not do. She tucks it behind his ear. He glances up, eyes flashing. Catching her hand as she makes to pull away, he brushes his lips against the heel of her palm.

"Let me stay," he whispers brokenly. "Let me be yours and you mine. Cinnia, I love you."

The world suddenly rushes by. Her body rocks with her thundering pulse, and she's floating, though her feet haven't left the ground. The faintest moan slips out from her mouth. His hands are on her arms again. He's shivering, clearly wanting to crush her against him, yet he resists, treating her with such care that she cannot help but smile. He's waiting for a sign. He will not take what she won't freely give. Beautiful boy. This alone would make her love him if she did not already.

But she does. Of course she does. Almost from the moment they met, she has loved him as though her soul had always been searching for his. She's found herself in him, just as in the water. He has restored those parts of her stolen by the fire. She wants to thank him, wants to whisper those three sacred words back to him, but words will never be enough. So she stares into his eyes while her fingertips explore every angle of his darling face. They have always used silence to speak to one another, and from the way he sighs, she's certain he has heard her.

Her hands move to his neck, fingers tangling in his tousled hair. His hands move to the small of her back, fingers curling in her woollen dress. As newborn stars twinkle amidst the candied sky, Cinnia and Eoin's lips meet, delicately yielding to each other, soft as silk and sweet as summer rain. They part as slowly as they came together, spellbound, lingering in the splendour of purest magic.

It won't be an easy life. There will always be days full of grief and nights lost to fear. They will never fully shake themselves free of the devils weighing them down, but even in the midst of darkness, they'll find light. They will mine it from their shared heart; thick, rich veins of it against which the wealth of a thousand kingdoms will appear worthless in comparison. The moon will never shine as bright as her eyes do when she looks upon him. The sun will never be as warm as his smile is when he holds her. And neither will have any more need for imagined lives or whispered wishes, for they have already found their happily ever afters in each other's love.

THE END

ABOUT THE AUTHOR

SARAH-JANE LEHOUX was a shy yet outspoken child whose irrepressible imagination often put her at odds with the world. She was never satisfied with the status quo, and now, as a writer of feminist speculative fiction, she isn't afraid to take chances or to tackle subjects that others may avoid. Because of this, her stories have been praised for their gritty realism and psychological insights, as well as their vivid imagery and originality.

Sarah-Jane has a BA in Anthropology from Laurentian University and a diploma in Animal Care from Sheridan College. She was a bit of a nomad in her youth, moving from one Canadian city to the next, before realising she needed a slower pace of life to truly be happy. She resides in Northern Ontario with her husband, her cats, and her books and spends her time cluttering her brain with beautiful nonsense. To learn more, please visit sarah-janelehoux.com

ALSO BY SARAH-JANE LEHOUX

THIEF
SHADES OF WAR
MASQUERADE
MY SANCTUARY

www.ingramcontent.com/pod-product-compliance
Lightning Source LLC
Chambersburg PA
CBHW020144120726
47903CB00007B/2413